# Dragonbound V

# Silver Dragon

Rebecca Shelley

Wonder Realms Books

ISBN-13: 978-0692278420

ISBN-10: 0692278427



Published by Wonder Realms Books

**For Abigail.**

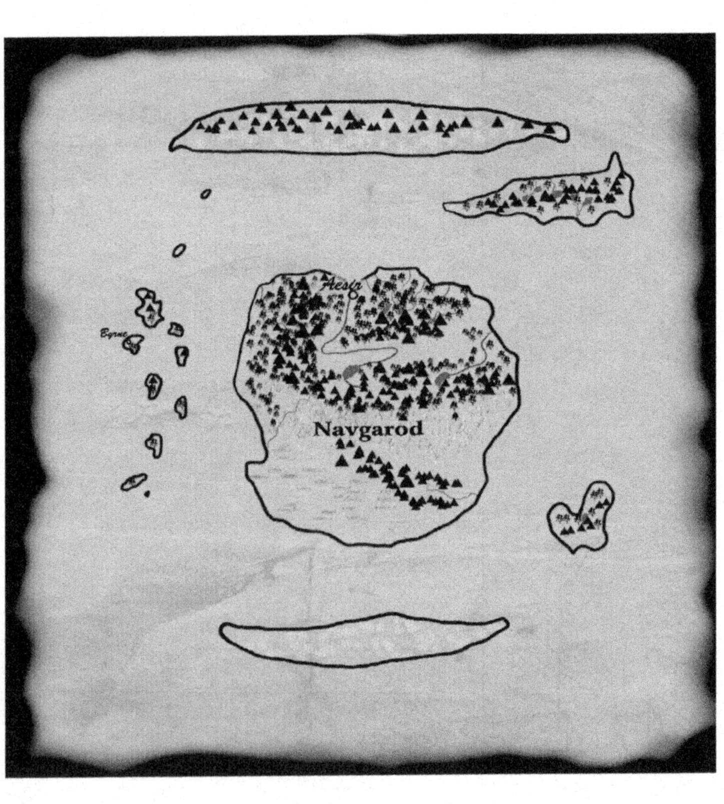

Aesir
Byrne
Navgarod

**Dragonbound**

Dragonbound: Blue Dragon
Dragonbound II: White Dragon
Dragonbound III: Copper Dragon
Dragonbound IV: Red Dragon
Dragonbound V: Silver Dragon

# Prologue

**Amar hurried through the** golden corridors, his robes rustling around him like shivers of fear. His heart beat hard in his chest. Something was wrong—Rajahansa was so angry, arguing with Dharanidhar again. He'd shut Amar out and would not listen. A stifling breeze blew through the great arched windows overlooking the jungle, but Amar barely gave it any notice as he rushed into Dharanidhar's chambers.

Parmver's surviving two sons and their dragons stood beside Rajahansa, confronting Dharanidhar. Parmver stood to one side, looking between them with worry, or was it fear.

*Get out!* Rajahansa roared at Dharanidhar. *You and Kanvar are no longer welcome here.*

"Yes they are," Amar had to yell to be heard above the roar and hiss of angry dragons.

Rajahansa pivoted to face him. His wings extended, his teeth bared in a feral snarl. *Stay out of this, Amar.*

"No. Kanvar is my son. Of course, he and Dharanidhar are welcome here."

*No longer. Kanvar has gone against my direct orders not to interfere with the Maranies. He and his friend Raahi have put us all in danger. Worse, he has taken my own son with him. To his death, no doubt.*

Amar spread his hands, trying to calm his dragon. "Kanvar said no one was hurt. Bensharie is fine. They are probably on their way back here right now."

*That is not the point. The point is he defied me. He disobeyed a direct command. Many of us will die because of it. What he has done is treason. He deserves worse than banishment.*

"He is under no obligation to follow your orders." Sweat broke out on Amar's forehead. He could not longer see into Rajahansa's mind. His lifetime friend and companion had shut him out. And something had changed. Something in the way he carried himself more regally, something in the way he spoke to others as if he thought himself more important than they, something in his heart had turned cold, and that frightened Amar more than anything else.

*I am the king!* Rajahansa lifted his head and let out a roar that echoed off the chamber walls, across the sky, and down into the jungle.

"King of what!" Amar shouted. "We have no kingdom, Rajahansa. All we have is this palace. We have no subjects. All we have is family. And you can't banish family."

*Kanvar is a cripple. He should have been killed at birth. But he wasn't, and his abomination will bring the death of us all. Already he has bonded with our worst enemy.* Rajahansa pointed a glittering claw at Dharanidhar who had risen up on his hind legs and spread his wings in answer to Rajahansa's challenge. *But that is not enough for him, no. He tries to make friends with the humans. He has betrayed knowledge of us to the leader of the Maran armies. They will come for us, and they will kill us unless we raise an army to fight them. But we cannot do that with a traitor among us who will tell all our plans to our enemies. Dharanidhar must go. He and Kanvar will be our doom.*

"Raise an army? Fight the Maranies? What are you saying? You're a gold dragon. What about peace? What about not killing living things? How could you even think to do what you're suggesting?" Goose bumps broke out on Amar's arms, and his gut twisted. "What sickness has taken your mind, old friend, that you would even think like this?"

*It is not a sickness. Your son has caused this. Your son has ruined everything for us. I'm just doing what must be done to keep us alive. We are the last gold dragons. The last Nagas. The humans will kill us if we don't defend ourselves.*

A dry laugh from Dharanidhar cracked across the hall. *I hear myself in your words, Rajahansa. All those years I fought the humans, and you tried to tell me I should not. And now, you suddenly agree with me, now that I have finally come to believe you that we should have peace?*

*Don't you dare talk to me, you old wyrm. It is your evil that has brought this war upon us. You must leave now, and if you ever come back, I will kill you.*

*You think you can? I think not.* Dharanidhar took a step back and sucked in a breath to stoke his fires. *I was born fighting, I will happily die the same way and take you out with me.*

"No. No, no no." Amar rushed out between the two dragons. "You'll kill me. You'll kill Kanvar. Please stop."

*You can't stop this,* Dharanidhar said.

Rajahansa snatched Amar up in his claw and set him to the side. *I am sorry, Amar. If Dharanidhar won't go peacefully, I will have to kill him.*

"He can't go peacefully," Parmver spoke up. "He can't see, Rajahansa. You know he can't. Not without Kanvar."

Amar's mind raced. His face grew hot. He'd hoped he would be able to talk reason into Rajahansa, but it seemed words could not do it. "Don't fight!" he shouted once more. "If Dharanidhar and Kanvar are banished, if Dharanidhar must go, then I will fly with him. I will be his eyes so he can fly away."

*You would betray me? You would side with our enemy?* Rajahansa said. The shock and hurt of Amar's words twisted Rajahansa to so much pain Amar could feel it through his shields.

"I'm not betraying you. I'm trying to follow your wishes. You want him gone. He can't go without help. I am helping him. I am trying to please you," Amar pleaded, trying to calm Rajahansa.

Rajahansa roared in frustration but dropped to all fours and backed away from Dharanidhar.

Amar walked over to Dharanidhar. "Please, Dhar, you don't need to fight. We are family. Let me fly with you. I will be your eyes as you fly back to your pride."

Dharanidhar shook his head.

Rajahansa growled.

Amar's mind swam. What about Kumar Raza's family? If Amar left, who would look after them? Who would make sure Rajahansa didn't turn on them as well? The family of a dragon hunter would be next on Rajahansa's purge list.

*I'll handle it*, Devaj spoke into his mind as he stepped into the room followed by his dragon. *Elkatran and I will take Eska and Denali to the jungle village.*

Amar nodded. "Pick me up, Dharanidhar." He opened his mind to the Great Blue dragon so Dhar could see through his eyes. Dharanidhar lifted him up onto his back and turned to face Rajahansa. *I wish no war with you, Rajahansa. If I am no longer welcome here, then I will leave. Amar is gracious to allow me a way to do it. I will see that he is safe.*

Rajahansa folded his wings and laid sad eyes on Amar. *I am sorry, Amar.*

"So am I, my friend. I will return as soon as possible. Then you and I will talk things over in a calmer manner. I'm sure we can come to some agreement."

Dharanidhar leaped out the window and winged down toward the jungle. The sudden lurch and jarring motion of Dharanidhar's body almost unseated Amar. He reached for the blue ridge scales, but they were smooth and he slid, almost falling. Dhar reached up and caught him and carried him in his claw instead.

*Oops, sorry. Forgot I wasn't wearing Kanvar's flying harness,* Dharanidhar said.

Amar swallowed his fear and focused on letting Dharanidhar see clearly through his own eyes. Through the link, he could feel the dragon's pain in his lower legs and the hurt of his wing that had never healed right. *What will you do without Parmver's medicine?* Amar asked.

Dharanidhar did not respond.

*Perhaps I can have Devaj bring you some from time to time.*

*Rajahansa will see that as treason and turn on him. You must leave me be as I am. As soon as I land, have one of the gold dragons come carry you back to the palace.* A sharp pain stabbed Dharanidhar's wing, and Amar felt it in his mind. Dharanidhar faltered and tipped dizzyingly before righting himself.

Amar winced and his stomach coiled tight. *Do you think the other blue dragons will try to harm you or me when we fly up to your home?*

Dharanidhar groaned and, instead of turning toward the high mountains, he flew above the jungle toward the shore.

*You don't think you can make it that far?* Amar asked.

*If we went to the Great Blues' nesting grounds they would kill me for sure, and you would likely die in the battle as well.* Dharanidhar flapped, lopsided and in pain, skimming around a mountain he could not hope to fly over.

*What?*

*I am in exile. Great Blue dragons do not grow old and infirm. They die in the blazing glory of battle. I am old and crippled. It was time for a younger, stronger leader. But I chose exile because Kanvar is still young. He should not die when his life has just begun.*

Amar leaned against the massive claw that held him. The ancient blue scales felt icy against his skin. His whole life seemed to have spun upside down. *But if you are not with the blue dragon pride, the younger dragons cannot hunt for you. How will you eat?*

*They would never hunt food for me like they did for Akshara. He was different. He was the Liberator. I am just an old dragon who has lived past my usefulness.*

*You can't be that much older than Rajahansa.*

*Perhaps we are equal in age, but he has lived a sheltered life. I have not.* Dharanidhar came around the edge of the mountain, and the emerald jungle stretched out to meet the azure ocean. He winged toward the shore. *Look there, that cove there where the jungle trees meet the sand, that is where the*

*Maranies murdered my mate and hatchlings. And those cliffs there, which wrap their arms around the cove to give it shelter, that is where the Great Blue dragon pride used to dwell. I will not go hungry here, even blind. I know this cove well. I will feed on seals and sea lions, dolphins and dragonfish once again. Kanvar and I have already moved my things to this place.* Dharanidhar swooped over the cove, winged out across the water, then swung back to the cliffs and settled to the ground near the opening of a cave.

Amar staggered as Dharanidhar set him onto the sand. Sunlight glittered off the black rock of the cave opening which had been carved to look like the grand arch into some king's great hall. If the fluted columns carved out of the rock on either side had been covered with gold, they would have been in place at the golden palace. Amar stepped closer and saw that intricate leafy vines and flowers had been carved around the columns as if they had grown there. He rubbed his fingers over the rock, expecting it to be rough like any volcanic cliff, but it was smooth and warm.

*Akshara was an artisan of stone. This is his lair and he carved it to suit himself. Step inside, you will see more.* Dharanidhar waited for Amar to stride into the cave before following.

Amar stepped into the cave and found that matching columns in crossed spirals held up the vast cavern. He gasped. "Dharanidhar I . . . I . . ."

*You thought the Great Blue dragons were merely barbaric savages?* Dharanidhar snorted. *Who do you think built the golden palace at Stonefountain and so many other mansions in that city? The gold dragons may have come up with the structural designs, but it was the blue dragons who raised the halls and etched the stone. And Akshara, he was the master carver. No one equaled his skill and creativity. But as Khalid's heart grew wicked, Akshara refused to work for him anymore. That is when Khalid chained him in the palace, took control of his mind, and forced him to continue his work.*

Dharanidhar sighed and sank to the ground in the middle of the chamber where the two sets of columns spiraled together into a central circle. *Look closely at the walls, they tell the story. Start on the left of the door there.*

Sunlight, streaming in from outside, illuminated the walls near the entrance. Carved in intricate detail was the history of the rise of Stonefountain. Amar watched it unfold on the wall as he walked around the cavern. On the wall farthest from the entrance, the stone fell into shadow as Khalid came into power, killing, coercing, enslaving. The stone pictures were so detailed as to be lifelike, the people moving and speaking, slaves crying in pain and fear. Amar realized he was seeing the abomination Stonefountain had become as a living memory in Dharanidhar's mind at the same time he took in the carved retelling of events. He heard the cry of an infant and glanced down near the base of the wall to see a newborn boy, deformed much like Kanvar, thrust naked onto a stone slab, Khalid raised the golden sword over him as if to strike, and in Dharanidhar's mind the vivid memory of the Khalid's arms slicing downward, silencing the baby forever.

"No." Amar dropped to his knees and buried his face in his hands, blocking out the images on the wall and raising a shield between his own mind and the pictures of Stonefountain in Dharanidhar's.

*It was long ago*, Dharanidhar whispered into his mind. *Things are different now.*

"Are they?" Amar rose and strode away from the wall to the center of the chamber where Dharanidhar lay. "You heard what Rajahansa said, that Kanvar should have been killed. He called him an abomination. Dharanidhar, why has the past come back to haunt us now, now when everything seemed to be so perfect?"

*I do not know. I only wish I were stronger. Rajahansa would not dare say something like that to my face while I was in my prime. He knows I could kill him before the words even formed in his mind.*

"It's not like him to say them at all, then or now. Something is wrong, Dhar, something has changed him." Amar shuddered and smoothed his robes.

Dharanidhar rumbled in agreement. *It is fear, most likely, fear of what the humans will do to you if they find you. Fear does strange things to a person. You must go back to him and help him overcome this fear. Make him see reason. Remind him of himself somehow.*

"But you are hurt and hungry."

*I'll be fine, and Kanvar will come back soon. You have more to worry about than me. Think of the others: Devaj, Denali, your wife and Kumar's. And that village girl, Tana. She will have to bond soon. You cannot leave her alone with Rajahansa while he is in such a mood.* Dharanidhar waved Amar toward the entrance. *I don't need to fly to move around and hunt here in the cove. Go. Be the king you're supposed to be.*

Amar glanced one more time at the walls, shuddered, and strode out of the cave, calling for Rajahansa to come get him.

## Chapter One

**Kanvar stared at the** Maran warships on the horizon. They were far behind the lifeboat where he sat with Rajan and Kumar Raza but getting closer every minute. The Maranies must have caught sight of the boat as it was leaving the island—a tiny indecipherable speak of brown bobbing on the heaving waves. Kanvar had hoped he could slip past the Maran war fleet without being noticed. It seemed not. Now the wind was on the Maranies' side. Soon the warships would catch up to them. The tap and scrape of Raza cleaning the hardened magma from his armor wound Kanvar's nerves in knots.

"I think they're gaining on us," Kanvar said. A biting wind had picked up from the rear, and the choppy up and down motion of the waves made him queasy.

"Why are they following us?" Rajan asked. "The whole Maran war fleet out after one little life boat?" Blood stained his shirt from the chest wound he'd taken as the Great Red dragon died.

Kanvar hadn't been able to keep himself from staring at the drying blood and the scar on Rajan's right cheek that Kanvar had caused, wielding his father's sword against the red dragon. Rajan had aged so much slower than Kumar Raza, who had a touch of gray in his flaming blond hair. Their faces were identical, except Kumar Raza's was tanned and worn with age while Rajan's was pale and young. He didn't look much older than Kanvar.

"You're a Naga, Rajan," Kumar Raza answered. "So is Kanvar. Do you suppose there is anyone in the whole world besides me that doesn't want you dead?"

Kanvar grinned. "Not to mention—"

"Stop." Kumar Raza pointed the chisel he'd been using to scrape his armor at Kanvar. "He's a Naga. That's enough."

Kanvar bit his lip and turned away. He wanted to argue with Kumar Raza that Rajan needed to know what he'd done to anger the Maranies. Taking control of the Maran government was no small thing. Or the fact that he had almost conquered Varna as well and was only moments away from ruling the world before Kanvar stopped him. But Kumar Raza had insisted that Kanvar erase those memories from his twin brother's mind. Kanvar had not yet admitted that he had only locked the memories up instead of destroying them completely.

"What is it? What aren't you telling me?" Rajan shivered and looked back at the advancing Maran warships with glassy eyes.

He's trying to remember, Kanvar realized. "Grandfather, I think Rajan needs to know."

Kumar Raza dropped his tools and grabbed Kanvar by the shoulders, barely stopping short of shaking him. "You … will … not!"

A gust of wind slammed the life boat from behind. Bensharie, the young gold dragon who had been flying in front of the boat, pulling it through the water to outrun the warships, gave a startled yelp and tumbled into the ocean. He thrashed for a moment in the water and then came head-up to the surface to float and rest. The sunlight slid off his golden plates, making him almost invisible, a trait all Great Gold dragons possessed.

*I'm sorry*, he said into Kanvar's mind. *I'm tired. The wind is making it hard. I have to rest.*

Kanvar twisted out of Kumar Raza's grasp and glanced back at the warships. The wind was full in their sails now, and the ships were coming on fast. "Grandfather."

"I know. I see it. Is Silverwave strong enough to pull now?"

Silverwave, the Great Silver serpent who had taken the bond with Rajan to keep him alive, grabbed the rope harness from Bensharie and started pulling the boat in his place. But her movements were sluggish in the water. She'd experienced with Rajan the weapon strikes that had killed the red dragon and had a matching scar on her chest to prove it. She'd been hurt badly in the ordeal and been holding onto the boat, letting Bensharie do all the work. Now she tried, but in her weakened condition, she was no match for the speed the wind gave the Maranies.

Kanvar stood and wiped the salty ocean spray from his blue dragonscale armor. "We need time for Bensharie to rest."

"Kanvar, sit back down," Kumar Raza said.

Kanvar shook his head, unbuckled his father's sword and laid it in the bottom of the boat next to the cookpot that contained Akshara's singing stone. Then he grabbed the satchel that carried the Great Red dragonstone and slung it over his shoulders. "I've got to go talk to General Chandran. He needs to know what's happened."

"You can't go back there," Kumar Raza protested.

"Yes I can. Especially if it means you and the dragons get away." He leaped into the water and started to swim toward the warships.

His strokes were broken and uneven because of his deformed leg and arm. The satchel dragged him down more than he expected. He floundered and his head went under for a moment. He held his breath, called for Silverwave, and forced his good arm and leg to stroke harder until his head came back up. Behind him in the boat,

Kumar Raza yelled for Silverwave to stop him. A moment later, cool silver coils wrapped around Kanvar and held him, stopping his movement.

Kanvar spit salt water out of his mouth. "Silverwave, you have to take me to the flagship back there."

*Kumar told me to stop you.* Silverwave's thoughts were sweet and tender as always.

"I must speak with Chandran."

*He'll kill you.*

"Not before I give him my message, and once I've done that, he'll stop chasing the life boat. Now help me. I must get to the warships before they get close enough to see clearly who is in the boat."

*You're planning something?*

"Yes, Silverwave, now please let's go."

Silverwave's coils tightened around Kanvar, then she swam through the water toward the advancing warships, carrying Kanvar with her. Behind them, Kanvar could hear Kumar Raza swearing. His sharp words matched the fear in Kanvar's heart. Kumar Raza was right. Chandran would have no choice but to kill Kanvar, but if it would buy Rajan's life it was worth the sacrifice.

Silverwave carried Kanvar just outside of the flagship's harpoon range, then she left him and dove under the water where the Maranies could no longer see her.

Kanvar took a deep breath and started to swim once more, but with the cumbersome satchel, he couldn't do much more than stay afloat until the flagship hove up beside him. The Maranies threw him a rope, which he tied around himself.

The rope tightened and he broke free of the water as the Maranies pulled him up. Halfway to the main deck, the piercing wail of two singing stones cut through his mind. Though Kanvar had cast Chandran's singing stone into the channel between Varna and Maran, General Chandran had not come hunting Nagas without procuring more.

The Maranies got him over the rail, and he fell to the deck on his knees, dripping water, his head aflame with the pain of the song from the stones. A pair of blue dragon-hide boots stepped in front of him. He knew those boots. He'd polished them often enough during the five years he'd spent as Chandran's indentured servant.

"Bind him," Chandran commanded.

The Maran soldiers dragged Kanvar to his feet, tore the satchel from him, and tried to tie his hands behind his back.

"That doesn't usually work too well." Kanvar lifted his gaze to look Chandran in the face.

The wind feathered Chandran's gray hair. His eyes held a mixture of pity and determination. Kanvar could not see into his mind; the singing stones held by two Maran dragon hunters prevented it.

The soldiers fumbled with Kanvar's stumpy left hand for a moment before realizing it would not reach behind his back to be bound to his right arm.

Chandran let out a single bark of laughter before taking the rope from his men, tying it to Kanvar's right wrist, wrapping it tight around his waist, and securing it back on the right wrist, immobilizing Kanvar's good hand.

Once he had Kanvar bound, Chandran's wrinkled cheeks grew red with anger. "You betrayed me, Kanvar."

Kanvar's throat was raw, but he forced himself to speak. "No. I did exactly what I told you I would do. I stopped the Naga. He broke our laws, we claim justice upon him."

"What justice would a Naga give another Naga? You saved him from a just Maran execution. You are a criminal, and you will pay for it with your life."

"I was born a criminal, Chandran. Born a Naga, which makes me subject to death by your laws through no actions of my own. But I risked my life anyway to help you, to save you from being enslaved. Do what you must with me, but first let me tell you what judgment has been executed upon the Naga I pulled from your grasp."

Chandran drew his sword. "Speak quickly. You don't have long to live."

Kanvar licked his lips and shuddered. He didn't like having his good hand bound so tightly. "The Naga was taken in his youth by a Great Red volcanic dragon who forced a bond with him against his own wishes. You know how cruel and bloodthirsty Great Red dragons are. The dragon found Naga power within his grasp and he took it, enslaving the Naga in a life of torment and agony. I saw into the Naga's mind, saw the horrors he survived. It took many years for the red dragon to learn to use and control the Naga's powers, and when he was ready, he sent the Naga to take control of the Maran government. Then he tried to use the Maran army to immobilize the Varnan dragon hunter jati while he usurped control of Varna as well. From there he planned to reestablish the kingdom at Stonefountain with himself as king. A Great Red dragon in control of the whole world. No mere handful of human slaves to torment and eat in his lair. He would have all the human flesh he wished. All the world enslaved to him. A Great Red Dragon King."

Kanvar shuddered. The thought was too horrible to imagine.

"Then why didn't you let me execute the Naga? That would have ended them both," Chandran snapped.

Kanvar sucked in a breath. He felt himself shaking as he tried to push Rajan's memories back into the dark corners of his mind, but the singing stones jumbled his thoughts in stabbing pain. "Because Great Red dragons keep human slaves. I could not stand the thought of those humans starving to death in the dragon's cages. I needed the Naga to lead me to the dragon so I could free them."

"And did you … free them?"

"Yes, and I brought you the proof. There in the satchel. The humans are free. You should pick them up from the island back there. The Great Red dragon is dead. The Naga has paid the price for his crimes along with him." The taste of salt water like blood and death clung to Kanvar's lips.

The soldiers untied the satchel, pulled the top back, and lifted the giant red dragonstone from its folds. A gasp went up from the soldiers and sailors that had gathered on deck.

"I did not betray you, Chandran," Kanvar said. "I did exactly what I told you I would. I stopped the Naga. I saved your life. Do with me what you will, but I wanted you to know the truth."

Chandran cleared his throat and twisted his wrist so his sword flashed in the sunlight. "You expect me to believe that you killed a Great Red volcanic dragon?"

"The Naga was bound hand and foot. I am good with a crossbow. Human flesh is not as impenetrable as red dragon scales."

Chandran pressed the tip of his sword against Kanvar's chest. "I am even less likely to believe you killed someone in cold blood than you killed a Great Red dragon. I know you too well, Kanvar."

Kanvar tensed and glanced at the two dragon hunters Chandran had brought with him. Somehow Kanvar had to explain without making his grandfather look like a friend of the Nagas. They could not have helped but see Kumar Raza in the boat with Kanvar as they fled the Maran capital. But Kanvar hoped he'd gotten to the warships in time that they could not now see Kumar Raza and Rajan in the tiny boat bobbing on the waves so far away.

Chandran pressed harder with his sword, and Kanvar knew at this range Chandran's hand was strong enough he could thrust the sword through Kanvar's armor. "Tell me the truth."

Kanvar nodded toward the red dragonstone. "There is only one man who can kill a Great Red dragon. He hunted me on the coast of Varna and caught me after I had taken the other Naga from you. He insisted we must go free the human slaves. And he, just for the sport of it, killed the red dragon instead of striking down the Naga. He would have killed me as well, but I grabbed the dragonstone and escaped while he was freeing the human slaves."

"Kumar Raza," the dragon hunters said in unison.

Kanvar nodded. "Raza."

Chandran lifted the sword away from Kanvar's chest. "And you expect me to believe he let you escape, just like that, and take the dragonstone with you?"

Kanvar choked. "He-he was distracted looking for the cages that held the human slaves. I got my hands on the singing stones, his and yours, and got them out of the way. When he returned from freeing the humans . . . he could not stop me."

Chandran swore under his breath and looked back to the west where they'd left the island behind. Then he looked down at the water below the boat. "We saw a Great Silver serpent with you. A friend of yours, I suppose, or a slave."

"A friend."

Chandran nodded. "Did you harm Kumar Raza?"

"No. I just ran away. He called me some very pointed names and introduced me to a few new swear words on my way out." Kanvar had to work hard not to smile fondly at the image of his grandfather in the life boat swearing at him as Silverwave carried him away.

"*You*, ran?" Chandran glanced meaningfully at Kanvar's deformed leg.

"I escaped in the boat. The serpent has been pulling it. But the Great Dragon Hunter is smarter than I thought. He sabotaged the boat, so it foundered. I should have known he wouldn't let me go so easily. I thought I'd outwitted him, but he knew I would get out into the open ocean and drown."

"Why didn't you just fly away on that devil of a gold dragon of yours?" one of the dragon hunters said, fingering his loaded crossbow.

Kanvar flinched and his mind went blank for a moment. He hadn't thought about that.

"Well," General Chandran demanded. "Where's your dragon?"

Kanvar's thoughts spun. Chandran knew he was bound to Dharanidhar, not a gold dragon. Though it seemed the dragon hunters assumed Bensharie was Kanvar's dragon. Kanvar wasn't sure which dragon Chandran was asking him about.

"T-the gold dragon is just a child, like me. He can't carry me far at his best, and the Great Dragon Hunter shot him. Twice. He does know how to swim though." Kanvar glanced out across the heaving ocean waves. The bright sun sent ripples of gold light across the water. The way the sun played on the waves in broad daylight, even the best of dragon hunters would not be able to pick out a gold dragon.

"Very well, Kanvar," General Chandran said. "I thank you for your help in freeing Maran from the red dragon and his Naga. Unfortunately, I must still sentence you to death. Our laws hold firm. All Nagas must die." He motioned to his men. "Get the plank."

"Wait," one of the Naga hunters said. "Before you kill him, I've got to know, how did Kumar Raza kill the Great Red dragon? He would never tell any of us his method. Tell me, Naga, or I'll make sure Chandran kills you in the slowest most painful way possible."

Kanvar shuddered and inched backward. "He … he hid by the pool of magma while the dragon was bathing in it. Then when the dragon came out all soft and hot, he drove a heavy harpoon into its heart and followed it up with a second harpoon through its eye into its brain. I can still see Raza's hands, his gauntlets red hot as they rammed the harpoon past its burning scales. I would never want to be that close to a Great Red dragon. Even wearing armor, he must have been burned, but he had dragon saliva with him, so I imagine he healed up all right."

The dragon hunters looked at each other and laughed. "Of course. Why didn't we think of that?"

Chandran's soldiers set a plank up on the side of the boat and lifted Kanvar onto it.

Chandran, sword still drawn, leaped up onto the plank and forced Kanvar out over the water to the end. The biting wind whipped their hair, stinging Kanvar's face. Chandran put a hand on his shoulder and spoke in a whisper. "Maran and Varna have made a pact to destroy your nest of Nagas in Kundiland. When I return, we sail together, the combined strength of our two armies and the skill and knowledge of the complete dragon hunter jati. Raahi let slip how to find the jungle village and that the gold dragons can be summoned from there. Your family and friends will die if you do not warn them."

"Chandran, no, please." Kanvar tried to pull away. Behind him, the ocean waves rolled.

Chandran held him tight, pressed the tip of his sword against Kanvar's gut, and spoke in a loud voice so the entire ship could hear. "Naga, I sentence you to death." He stabbed the sword through Kanvar's gut, then pulled it free, and pushed Kanvar off the plank, letting him fall into the cold waves.

## Chapter Two

**"What are they going** to do to him?" Rajan squinted at the boats.

"They'll kill him, of course." Kumar Raza slipped his armor on and put his tools away replacing them with his crossbow. He handed his sword to Rajan. "Here you go, brother, you were always better at the sword than I was anyway."

"What good will it do? We can't fight the whole army." Rajan curled his fingers around the sword hilt. The familiar weapon felt good in his hand, and he wondered what had happened to his own sword. It had ended up in the Great Red dragon's hoard, no doubt. Thinking about the sword did little to make him feel better about Kanvar swimming off to sacrifice himself in an attempt to save them.

"We don't have to fight the whole army. We just have to keep them distracted while Bensharie snatches him off the deck. Bensharie, get up," Kumar Raza called. "You have to take us back to get Kanvar."

*Kanvar knows what he's doing,* Bensharie said without lifting off from the waves.

"Stupid dragon," Kumar said. "I guess we swim. You feel up to swimming, brother?"

Rajan fastened the sword belt around his waist. It seemed his brother was not a Naga and could not hear the dragon voices. "I like swimming. Let's go."

Kumar dove into the water, but before Rajan could join him, Silverwave spoke into his mind. *No. Wait there. I've got him.*

"Kumar," Rajan called. "Silverwave says to wait here. She's got him."

Off in the distance, the sails snapped, and the Maran warships swung around, tacking into the wind to head back the way they'd come. A few minutes later, Silverwave appeared. She had Kanvar in her coils and kept his head above water as she swam to the boat. She looped up and heaved him over the side. He slid to the bottom of the boat, shaking in pain, face pale. A blossom of blood spread from a stab wound in his gut.

"He's hurt," Rajan shouted.

Kumar climbed into the boat and knelt beside him. "Looks like they tied him up, stabbed him, and shoved him into the water, figuring he'd drown. Silverwave, I need you to lick this." Kumar cut Kanvar's bonds, unbuckled his armor, and tore it off.

Silverwave snaked her head over the side of the boat and licked the wound.

Rajan shook his head. "It's deep. Goes all the way through. It might have hit something vital."

Kumar Raza lifted Kanvar so Silverwave could lick at the wound from his backside, making sure the saliva went deep into the wound to heal all the way through.

Kanvar coughed and blinked his eyes open. "It didn't hit anything vital," he said in a cracked voice. "Chandran knew what he was doing."

"What do you mean?" Rajan didn't like seeing so much blood on someone who had so recently saved him from the red dragon.

"He had to make it look like he'd executed me. It's his job. But if he'd meant for me to die, he'd have stabbed me in the heart, and he was careful to be sure before he struck that Silverwave was a friend and waiting below, and Bensharie was out here somewhere. He's an old soldier. He knows what dragon saliva can do." Kanvar coughed again and then struggled up onto one of the benches. He was still shaking.

"Maybe you should stay lying down," Rajan said.

Kanvar shook his head. "Bad news, Grandfather. They kept the dragonstone." He flashed Kumar Raza a wicked smile.

Rajan sucked in a sharp breath. "Don't you know how much that is worth?"

"It's worth your life, Rajan, bought and paid for. See, the Maran warships are turning back." Kanvar rubbed the blood away from his healing wound. "I always wondered what it would feel like to be stabbed by a sword. Guess what? It hurts."

"Rajan's right. You should lie back down and rest. We all need rest now that we're safe," Kumar Raza opened his pack of supplies and pulled out food and water.

Kanvar sipped the water, but said his gut hurt too much to eat the fruit and crusty bread his grandfather offered him. "I can't rest here for too long," Kanvar said. "Chandran warned me that the combined Maran and Varnan armies are going after the other Nagas. He knows where the village is. I have to get back there first and get everyone moved to safety."

"He told you his plans?" Rajan said. "That doesn't make sense. Why warn your enemy when you could catch them by surprise and destroy them? Especially Nagas. Wait, there are other Nagas like us?" Rajan glanced over at the retreating warships.

"A few. In Kundiland. I have to get back there before he does. Bensharie, can you fly me home? Have you rested enough? I'm sorry to leave you, Grandfather, but you're safe now. Silverwave can take her time to recover and then swim you back to Kundiland." Kanvar slid into his armor and buckled it on. Then he secured his crossbow on his back and his father's sword at his waist.

*I can fly*, Bensharie said, *I've rested a bit now* and *carrying you will be easier than trying to pull the boat. My body wasn't built for towing.* His golden thoughts seeped into Rajan's mind as he spoke to Kanvar. Rajan rubbed his temples, not sure when he'd get used to dragons talking inside his head.

"Hold on," Kumar Raza said. "You can't fly back westward. Those warships will see you if a cloud covers the sun even for a moment."

"They have dragon hunters aboard," Kanvar said. "They don't need a cloud. They could see the ripple of sunlight as he flies. But we can stay close to the water where the sunlight always ripples. We have to get back to Kundiland. We'll have to risk flying past them and hope they don't notice."

"No, you don't." Kumar Raza rummaged around his pack and pulled out an ancient map. "Look at this. Devaj and I found it at Stonefountain." He unrolled the map, which looked nothing like any Rajan had ever seen.

"That doesn't make any sense," Rajan said.

"Yes it does; the world is round," Kumar Raza said. "If it weren't we would have sailed off the edge by now. But see, this side of the map is the world we know, and this other side is where we're sailing now. This chain of islands is somewhere in front of us, and that land mass, Navgarod the map calls it—bigger than Varna isn't it?—is where we'll go next. Then we'll have to skirt around the coast to get to the other side. From there it is straight east to reach the far coast of Kundiland."

"Amazing." Rajan ran his fingers over the ancient map, reveling in the smell of the vellum and the intricate hand that had scribed it. "We're sailing around the world. I don't believe it."

"I don't have time to skirt around the coast," Kanvar said. "Bensharie can fly me straight across that continent. If we don't run into a storm, we might just make it to Kundiland ahead of General Chandran. Bensharie, can you do it?"

*Yes. I might have to rest for a while when we reach land though. I can't fly it non-stop.* Bensharie spoke so both Kanvar and Rajan could hear him.

*Of course not*, Kanvar answered. He got to his feet and spoke to Kumar Raza. "When you reach Kundiland, stay hidden. Don't go to the village. I'll get in contact with you."

"Be careful Kanvar," Kumar Raza enveloped him in a stout hug. "And take Akshara's singing stone with you." He lifted the iron pot from the bottom of the boat, tucked it into a cloth bag with a strap, and looped it over Kanvar's shoulder then handed Kanvar a waterskin as well.

Kanvar grimaced and turned to Rajan. "I really shouldn't leave you. There is so much you need to learn. Your powers . . . you have to understand how to control them. And . . ." He glanced sideways at Kumar Raza then spoke directly into Rajan's mind so Kumar couldn't hear. *Your memories, he thinks I erased them, but I locked them away in your mind. There are things he does not want you to know, but someday you'll have to face them. It would be better if you and I could do that together.*

"I'll be all right," Rajan said. "I think." He rubbed his head, nervous all of a sudden about Kanvar leaving him alone with his brother. Kumar was no longer young and innocent, he no longer looked to Rajan to lead him. The tables had turned, and Rajan felt vulnerable. Kumar looked so much like their father, and that scared Rajan for some reason. He didn't know why. Fear of betrayal, hurt, and death cascaded through his mind.

"Rajan." Kanvar put his good hand on Rajan's shoulder. "Kumar is nothing like your father. He will never beat you for asking questions about your powers, never betray you. You can trust Kumar. Believe me, you can."

"You read my thoughts?"

"It's hard not to. You must remember to shield them. I know you can; you taught Kumar how to do it. You must concentrate, keep control of your mind and your powers. When you get to Kundiland, I'll introduce you to Parmver. He's the Naga who has been training me." Kanvar gave him a reassuring smile then climbed on Bensharie's back. Bensharie flapped his wings, and the sunlight rippled as he flew away.

Rajan slumped to the bench, blinking the bright light out of his eyes. "He's brave."

"Crazy brave," Kumar said, frowning and raking his fingers through his beard. "Chandran could just as easily have stabbed him through the heart. But then, Chandran practically raised Kanvar. They were like family."

A cold shiver ran up Rajan's spine, and he felt a flash of pain in his ribs. He looked down, sure he'd been struck by a crossbow bolt. There was none there, but the memory of his uncle shooting him felt as if it had happened that very moment. He gasped and pressed his hand to his side. "Family means nothing if you are a Naga."

Kumar's brow furrowed. "It means something to me, Rajan. I tried to save you."

"But you didn't know I was a Naga."

"Not at the time, but I found out later. And I swore I would never kill one of my own family for that reason. I looked for a long time to find the Great Gold dragons so my daughter would have someone to bond with if she came down with the fever. She never did, but while I was searching for the dragons, the Naga king found me. He married my daughter, and both of their children, Kanvar and Devaj, are Nagas. You need not fear family turning on you again, Rajan. You belong to a family of Nagas now. They will do anything to keep you safe, even confront the Maran general and take a sword in the gut for you."

"Naga king?" Rajan didn't like the sound of that.

"King Khalid's grandson. But don't worry, he's nothing like Khalid. Amar and I are friends. He's an excellent dragon hunter."

"He hunts dragons?"

"Lesser dragons, though he cheats horribly, using his powers to sense where they are." Kumar laughed. "You've never been on a real dragon hunt until you've hunted with the king."

Rajan ran his fingers along the smooth sword hilt at his waist. Sweat slicked his palms. "I did not think any Nagas had survived the destruction of Stonefountain, let alone one of the royal family. Everything I've been taught is screaming that I should be outraged. The Nagas are dangerous. They will try to enslave us all, just like Khalid did. But . . . how can I be a Naga? How can I live with myself? I should be dead."

"You want to die?"

"No." Rajan rubbed his head as if he could erase the truth of his existence from his mind. "I don't want to die. I just don't want to be a Naga."

"And the dung-raker who cleans the streets of Daro doesn't want to be a dung-raker, but he was born into that jati. It is his place in life. The untouchable does not want to be an untouchable. You were born a Naga. That is your position in life whether you would have it be so or not. Now stop fretting and eat." Kumar pressed some cheese and bread into his hand.

Rajan nibbled the cheese and stared back the way Kanvar had flown. "How do you think he convinced the warships to turn back?"

Kumar swallowed a chunk of bread before answering. "My guess is, he told them the red dragon was dead and let them believe you were dead with it. He had to give them the stone as proof. Then he allowed General Chandran to kill him. Both Nagas dead. Mission complete. They can all go home."

Rajan nodded in grateful appreciation for what Kanvar had done. With the ships gone, all around them lay water. No land in sight. Rajan felt isolated out in the middle of the water, but his fear of the endless expanse of heaving waves gave way to Silverwave's joy at swimming in the cool water. He felt her languid body looping and sliding, moving in an elegant dance of life amidst the ocean's currents. A sudden longing to join her in the water brought Rajan to his feet. He stepped toward the side of the lifeboat, but Kumar grabbed his arm.

"What are you doing?"

"I . . . just want to go swimming. Just for a minute. While Silverwave's resting."

"You're still weak."

"That's why I need the water. Need to be *in* the water. To be whole again. To feel safe." Rajan shrugged out of his shirt and trousers.

Kumar let go of him, but his brow wrinkled in a frown. "I suppose wanting to swim is better than wanting to bite me, but Rajan, try to remember you can't breathe underwater just because Silverwave can."

"Bite you?"

Kumar rubbed a scar on his cheek that looked suspiciously like it was made by human teeth. “It’s nothing. You were just a little eccentric while you were bound to the red dragon.”

“I bit you?”

Kumar waved the question away. “Go, swim. Have fun.” He settled back in the boat and closed his eyes.

Rajan stared at the bite marks on Kumar’s face and shuddered. His jaw tightened, and saliva filled his mouth. A strange hunger twisted his gut.

*Rajan?* Silverwave’s cool mind brushed against his.

*I bit him, Silverwave? Why do I taste the memory of blood on my tongue?*

*Let it go, Rajan. It’s over. You are no longer bound to that monster.* Silverwave sent a coil up over the boat. It wrapped around his middle and jerked him down into the water.

Rajan laughed as the shock of the cold water hit him. Sunlight sparkled like joy across the ocean as he and Silverwave played in the ocean’s embrace.

## Chapter Three

**"Sailing around the world** in a lifeboat, pulled by a Great Silver serpent, we never dreamed we'd have an adventure like this, eh Kumar?" Rajan knelt at the front of the boat and let the salty breeze slap his face as the boat crested a swell and came down into a trough. "All the boys back home will be so jealous."

Kumar snorted. "All the boys back home are grown into old men now. And yes, they're bound to be jealous. I've always outshone them, though I never intended to. Too bad you're a Naga, officially dead, and can't be there when I tell the dragon hunter council about this latest adventure. They probably won't believe me though, no one who ever sailed this far east has returned."

"By the fountain, you're right. How will I ever make my mark as a famous dragon hunter when I'm supposed to be dead? I know, I could take a new identity as your grandson." Rajan spun around to face his brother. Kumar looked old enough to be his grandfather.

"Won't work." Kumar lifted the waterskin to his lips, but only a drop trickled out. "The dragon hunter council knows both my grandsons are Nagas. That my daughter married a Naga. They think she killed all three of them herself."

"Maybe you had another child." Rajan scrabbled to find some sense of identity he could present to the world.

"I did, and he's a Naga. Young though. Only twelve. He hasn't come down with the fever yet." Kumar smiled wistfully. "He's a good boy."

Rajan leaned forward. "So? I could still be your son. Older. Born before him."

Kumar dropped the empty waterskin. "Rajan. You *cannot* go to Daro. They will recognize you, and they will kill you."

Kumar's words felt like he had struck Rajan in the face. He winced. "But . . . how could they, if I've been locked up in the red dragon's lair all these years?" He felt around in his mind, trying to find the memories that would confirm he'd been with the red dragon. He came up against a wall, thick, smooth, and blank.

Kumar growled under his breath. "Our water's gone. The food is gone. Ask Silverwave if she can tell how close we are to those islands."

"Who cares about food and water? Don't change the subject. You're hiding something from me, and I want to know what it is. Why can't I go to Daro? How could they possibly recognize me?" Rajan dug his nails into the wooden bench he sat on and wondered for a flash second why his claws could not tear the bench to splinters. He jerked his hands away. His eyes stung as he stared at his brother, but Kumar set his jaw and said nothing.

A feral growl sprang unbidden from Rajan's throat. He tried to spread his wings, leap across the boat, and sink his teeth into his brother's neck. But his leap only took him part way, and he landed flat on his stomach. The impact forced the air out of his lungs. He gasped but couldn't draw more in. Sliding off the bench, he curled into a ball on the floor of the boat.

"Rajan." Kumar knelt beside him and rubbed his back, forcing his lungs to open up and accept air. "Come on. Breathe."

Rajan managed to suck in enough air to moan. His mind spun from burning magma to cool ocean depths.

*Stay here with me*, Silverwave whispered into his mind. *We are cool water. We are peace.*

Rajan gritted his teeth, pulled away from his brother, and slipped over the side of the boat to join Silverwave. She caught him as he went under, and he wrapped his arms around her torso, letting her pull him to the surface where they skimmed along as she hauled the boat with his brother in it behind them.

Hours later an island came into view on the horizon. Rajan was chilled numb from the cold ocean, but he didn't want to get back into the boat with Kumar. He stayed with Silverwave until she crawled out of the water onto the rocky beach. A forest of pine trees covered mountain slopes above the water. A blast of cold air battered Rajan's face. He tried to walk, but his legs were too numb to carry him.

Kumar jumped out of the boat as soon as Silverwave drew it up onto the shore. He pulled Rajan's arm up over his shoulders and helped him stumbled away from the water into the trees. Neither of them said anything to each other as Kumar gathered wood and started a fire.

"Silverwave," Kumar called to the serpent who had coiled herself on the beach. "See if you can find a stream inlet along the coast close to here. We need fresh water."

Silverwave uncurled and returned to the water.

Rajan tried to get up to follow her, but Kumar restrained him with a strong hand on his shoulder. "Stay by the fire. You're wet and you're cold. You'll get hypothermia if you don't dry off and warm up." He checked the crossbow and bolts on his back. "I'm going to hunt us some dinner. Keep the fire going."

As Kumar strode away, Rajan edged closer to the fire and put his palms up to warm them. The sun was setting, and the forest would soon be dark. He strained to hear the sounds of the animals that must be lurking in the trees. He'd memorized which lesser dragons thrived in different habitats around the world, which ones on which continents, but this was a new place. Not so different really than the northern pine forests of Kundiland, right? He heard the chatter of squirrels, the chirp of birds. He listened more closely for the rasp of lesser brown raptor scales against tree bark. Though the raptors were only knee high, they hunted in packs and moved in silence through a forest. Only the rustle of leaves of the faint sound of their scales rubbing against the trees would give away their location. He glanced at the tree trunks around him and the branches overhead. They would come from all sides and from above. Their scales looked like tree bark. They could hold still on a trunk for hours waiting for their prey.

He saw no sign of the raptors, heard no sound that would forewarn an attack. "Be the hunter or be hunted," he reminded himself the lesson his instructors had drilled into his head. What else might be on this island? Black dragons or green dragons of various varieties, serpents in the streams and lakes.

A twig snapped behind him.

He drew his sword and jumped to his feet. He had no armor, only a flimsy linen shirt and trousers.

*What do we have here?* A thought swelled in his mind. *Smells human.*

A mottled gray and black shadow moved beyond the trees a dozen yards away. A Great dragon of some kind, since Rajan had heard its thoughts, not just impressions from its mind.

*I'm not human.* Rajan set his stance, in case the dragon attacked him. It was so well camouflaged he could not yet be sure of its shape and size.

A sharp hiss rattled the trees. It was big then, big enough Rajan wished he had Kumar's crossbow.

*A Naga? It has been long since a Naga has flown to these shores. But I do not smell a gold dragon with you.* The words rumbled through his mind, deep and ancient. He sensed the dragon now. It was big, but seldom moved far, content to let the forest creatures wander into range of its jaws to be snapped up in an instant.

*I'm bound to a silver serpent,* Rajan said.

*Impossible.*

*No, or I wouldn't be bound to her.*

*I thought the Nagas were extinct.*

*So did I.*

A shadow moved near the closest tree beside Rajan.

Rajan shifted to face it, sword raised.

Kumar stepped out, motioning for Rajan to be silent. He pointed into the shadows where the Great dragon lay and lifted his crossbow to take aim.

"No." Rajan leaped forward and grabbed the crossbow from his hands. "He's a Great dragon. Leave him alone."

Kumar shrugged. "Probably too big to eat anyway, but are you sure it's friendly?"

*Are you friend or foe?* Rajan asked the dragon.

A rumble of laugher like rocks rolling down a hill filled the forest.

*The Naga asks if I am a friend. I would ask the same of it, but I know it is not. I tell you, I will die before I become your slave.*

"My slave? I would not. Could not. What?" Rajan said aloud. He shoved Kumar's crossbow back into his hands and readied his sword.

*So you say.* Trees creaked and pine needles rustled as the old dragon got to its feet. It was huge. Dirt and plants that had grown on its back during its long years of immobility cascaded to the ground.

"We mean you no harm. We want nothing from you!" Rajan shouted. "Leave us alone, and we'll leave you alone."

The dragon spread its wings above the trees, and mottled black scales glinted in the setting sun. Its head snaked up as it bared its teeth.

"Do you suppose it breathes fire?" Rajan whispered to Kumar.

"Great Black forest dragon. Probably not. Can't you convince it we're not enemies?"

"You heard me try. It didn't work."

"You're a Naga, convince him."

"I'm a Naga. That's the problem. He—"

A spray of burning black goo shot from the dragon's throat. Rajan dove to one side, Kumar to the other. Rajan rolled to his feet and dodged behind a tree.

Kumar got a shot off with the crossbow that hit the dragon in its throat. "That ought to keep him from spraying tar for a moment."

The dragon let out a gurgling roar of pain and swatted at Kumar and Rajan with his heavy tail, knocking a row of trees over in the process. Rajan dropped to the ground, so the tail passed over top of him. Kumar jumped onto the tail as it swung past and ran up it onto the dragon's back.

"Make it stop, Rajan!" Kumar yelled. "I don't want to have to kill it." He aimed his second bolt at the dragon's eye as it twisted its head around to tear him off its back.

*Stop. Please stop*! Rajan spoke into the angry dragon's mind. *We're friends. I have not come to enslave you. I would never do that to anyone.*

*Liar!*

The dragon snapped its jaws toward Kumar. Kumar's finger moved on the trigger.

*"Stop! Both of you!"* Rajan shouted putting all his will and mental energy behind the command.

Both dragon and dragon hunter froze in place, a split second away from killing each other.

The rush of power made Rajan giddy. He sucked in a heated breath, realizing that he could control anyone, make them do anything. No one could stop him. He could make all the world bow to his commands. The dragon and his brother remained frozen in place. Neither could move without his permission. Neither could speak. The forest went dead still. For several long moments nothing moved.

*I can't breathe. Let me breathe*, the dragon's thoughts came as a desperate whisper into his mind. Rajan realized with horror that neither the dragon nor Kumar could breathe. He had stopped them completely. He could just as easily have stopped their hearts.

*"Breathe!"* he shouted. But his own breath caught in his throat. He could have killed them. Accidentally, with a single command. *"You may move, but neither of you will hurt each other from now on,"* he said. Then he left them and ran, back to the beach, back to the water, calling for Silverwave, frightened of himself, horrified by what he'd become.

He shivered as the chill evening air cut through his wet clothes. Silverwave was up the coast. It would take her a few minutes to reach him. He sheathed his sword, wrapped his arms around himself, and started walking, his teeth chattering. The round stones of the beach made his steps awkward and uneven. The ocean surf hissed and sprayed.

I'm a Naga, he thought. Power . . . so much power. Corrupts. I should be dead. What have I become? I cannot live with this. *Oh please, Silverwave, help me. I'm so cold. So lost.* He wished for Daro's sunshine and desert sand. For the happy chatter of shoppers in the street, the clucking of itchekins and the mewl of kitrats. He had a pet kitrat once, Little Ravi, cuddly scales and a tail that used to wrap around his arm when he carried him out of the house. I want to go home. I don't want to be a Naga. I'm a dragon hunter. I live in Daro. I have a twin brother my same age. This is all a dream, a nightmare. He splashed into a tide pool, twisted his ankle, and fell to his knees.

Strong arms lifted from the pool and embraced him. His brother's arms, grown so much bigger and older.

"It's all right, Rajan. Come back to the fire. You're freezing. No harm done. The dragon has settled back to sleep."

"No harm? How can you say that? I nearly killed you. Both of you. And . . . and . . . and just for a moment I thought I enjoyed it. I wanted to use my power. To control people. To hurt people. Kumar, please, just kill me now. I'm a monster. You can't trust me. I can't trust myself. There's something evil inside me. I can feel it." Rajan couldn't stop shaking. The cold wind seemed to wrap around his heart and freeze it.

"There was evil in you," Kumar's deep voice rumbled. "But I purged it. I killed the red dragon. It can no longer control you, no longer make you do things against your will."

Rajan shuddered. "I don't know what has happened. You've hidden it from me. I don't know what I've done. But what if I didn't do anything against my will? What if I wanted to be bound to the red dragon?" Pain of betrayal and hunger for revenge spread like ice crystals from his frozen heart. "You can't change the person I am inside. You can't make me a better man, just by changing what dragon I'm bound to."

"You're cold. Hypothermic. Talking nonsense. Now come with me back to the fire. We'll get you out of those wet clothes, wrap you up in a blanket, get some warm food in you, and you'll be fine. You'll get some rest, and tomorrow will be a better day." Kumar Raza forced Rajan back into the trees and over to the fire.

Rajan went along without further protest, but inside he doubted he'd be any better in the morning.

## Chapter Four

**Kumar Raza watched his** brother sleep, huddled in a blanket as close to the fire as he could get. Blue light seeped into the eastern sky. He should not have let Rajan stay in the water so long with his dragon. Human skin was not made to withstand so much cold. Stupid, Raza, he chastised himself. Do you want to kill your brother off so soon after finding him? Let him freeze to death? Poor Rajan.

Kumar tried to convince himself it had just been the cold talking with what Rajan had said the night before. Surely there could be no evil in his brother. They'd grown up together. Rajan had been willful, full of tricks and mischief, but never evil. He had a kind heart and a strong need to protect those who were weaker than him. But he'd spent decades bound to the red dragon. Was it possible that even with the memories gone, the dragon had warped Rajan's mind and personality, had changed him forever?

"No. It can't be." Kumar got to his feet and put out the fire.

Rajan groaned and opened his eyes to stare up at him. "Is it morning already?"

"I'm afraid so." Kumar set about ordering the supplies in his pack.

"I'm thirsty."

Kumar handed him a waterskin filled from a nearby river Silverwave had found.

Rajan drank and then glanced over to where the Great Black dragon had settled back to sleep. "We're lucky he didn't kill us while we were sleeping last night."

"You used your powers on him. I don't think he can," Kumar said.

"He can't kill you. I didn't say anything about not hurting me." Rajan rolled from his blanket and checked to see if his clothes had dried after Kumar had hung them by the fire.

"He hasn't moved."

"Maybe he's dead. You shot him in the throat."

"It wasn't a mortal wound, not for a Great dragon. His saliva healed it before he lay back down." Kumar hiked the pack onto his back, eager to get going. "Let's go."

"I can't . . . leave yet." Rajan got his clothes on, wrapped the blanket around his shoulders, and took a few steps toward the sleeping Great Black dragon. "I'm sorry," he called. "I didn't want to use my powers on you."

The dragon rumbled, and Kumar wished he could hear the dragon's thoughts like his brother could.

Rajan stood still for a long while as the two of them talked. Kumar waited, shut out from the conversation. Finally, Rajan shook himself and came back to Kumar. "He's very old. His parents were slaves at Stonefountain. I can't make him believe I'm any different than the Nagas back then."

"It doesn't matter as long as he's not trying to kill us."

"It matters to me." Rajan glanced over his shoulder at the dragon and then headed to the beach. "Silverwave says there's a fishing village a few miles from here. Small. Quiet. They hate Nagas."

"Doesn't everyone?"

"There's a statue of a Great Gold dragon on the hill overlooking the harbor. Silverwave thinks this was once a Naga outpost, but the statue now has a harpoon through the dragon's heart and an inscription that reads *Death to Those Who Come from the Sky.*"

"Lovely. I guess we should not mention that you're a Naga then." Kumar hoped Kanvar hadn't run into them.

"I think we should stay out of the village."

"We need supplies."

"We can hunt for our own food and get water up-stream from the village. There's no reason to go there."

"You need warmer clothes."

"Kumar, I'm not going anywhere near this place. If you have money, you can go into town for supplies. I'll wait in the forest."

Rajan was probably right to want to avoid the village, but Kumar hadn't slept more than just snatches here and there for so long, all the time on the water from Daro to the red dragon's island, and all the days since until they reached this one. He'd given Rajan most of the food and water on the boat, taking little for himself. And his muscles still ached from the battle with the red dragon. He wasn't young anymore, his body was no longer used to that much exertion. He needed to rest in the safety of a building with food and water and heat, and he couldn't go to the village and leave Rajan alone out in the forest. It wasn't safe for either of them.

"I can't just walk into the village out of nowhere," Kumar said. "They'll think I've come from the sky. We have to row the lifeboat in and tell them we were onboard a ship which sank. Cast adrift. Ended up here." Kumar got the lifeboat and pulled it toward the water. It scrapped across the rocks. "Come on Rajan, help me. This is heavy."

Rajan caught hold of the boat and helped him carry it. "You don't have to do this, Kumar. You can sleep. I'll stand guard. I'm warming up not that the sun is rising. We can stay away from the village."

"You reading my thoughts?"

"Yes, I'm reading your thoughts. I can't help it."

"My shields were up."

"Flimsy shields. You can't hide your mind from me, Kumar, you never could."

Kumar laughed. "No. That's why you always won when we played that dragon hunter game. But Rajan, we really do need the supplies and a safe place to sleep. You don't have to say anything. You don't have to talk to anyone. Just let me handle it, all right?"

They got the boat into the water, and Silverwave's head broke the surface. The dragonstone on her forehead flashed. Rajan laughed. Once again Kumar found himself jealous of his brother's rapport with the dragons. Why was I not a Naga? he wondered. Why can I only sense the dragons and never speak to them with my mind?

Rajan rubbed Silverwave's forehead then turned to him. "I'm sorry, Kumar."

"It doesn't matter." Kumar waved away his own resentment. "Silverwave, will you pull us up close to the village?"

Silverwave nodded and flashed under the water. In a moment, the boat began to move. An hour later, the village came into view with its ominously impaled gold dragon statue. "Now that *is* a pretty sight," Kumar said sarcastically. He pulled out the oars and handed one to Rajan. "Your face is sunburned enough they'll have to believe we've been out on the water for a while."

"We have been. So whose brilliant idea was it to travel around the world in a lifeboat? Oh, that's right. Yours."

Rajan dug in with the oar as Silverwave abandoned pulling them and vanished into the depths.

"Hey!" Kumar waved his oar and shouted as soon as they were within hearing distance of the docks. "Hey, help us, please!"

A couple of old fishermen who had been mending nets on the dock jumped to their feet. They threw Kumar a rope and helped pull the lifeboat up against the dock and secure it.

"Thank the fountain," Kumar said, rising to his feet. "I feared we would never find any land anywhere. Our water's gone, our food's gone, we've been drifting for so long I've lost count of the days. What is this place? Where are we?" He climbed up on the dock and grabbed the closest fisherman in a bear hug like a man truly thankful to be rescued.

"This village is called Bryne," the fisherman said. "You are very lost if you have come here. Few people seldom venture this far westward from the mainland."

"West from the mainland? What mainland?" Kumar said, feigning surprise. "The last mainland we saw was Darvat. We were hunting dragons in the Eastern Isles when our ship hit a shoal and sank. If we'd gone west we should have ended up back in Darvat."

The fisherman shook his head in bewilderment. "Darvat, why, that's on the other side of the world. But no one from the old land ever comes this way. The wind and tides are against it. Your lifeboat must have been caught up in some strange ocean vortex to end up here. Only the Naga lords ventured this far."

"Nagas?" Kumar shuddered. "Please tell me no Naga lord rules this place. I thought they were all dead a thousand years ago."

Still in the boat, Rajan moaned and buried his face in his hands.

"Come. There are no Nagas here." The second fisherman stepped down into the boat and urged Rajan to his feet. "Forgive us old men blathering when you need water and food."

"Thank you for your kindness," Kumar said. "My son has not fared well out there on the water for so long. He is thirsty and frightened."

Kumar helped Rajan up onto the dock, then grabbed his supply pack and followed the fishermen into the village. Two dozen houses were built on wooden pilings which allowed the tide to come and go beneath them. Wooden walkways connected the dock to the houses. The town smelled of salt water and fish, accented by the smell of pine logs burning in fireplaces. At the head of town, closest to shore, a long house spread its great hall. The villagers, dressed in warm woolen clothes, gathered as Kumar and Rajan entered. The hall was one long room with a blazing fire burning in a fire pit in the center. Tables and benches sat in a scattered oval around the fire.

"Thank you, thank you," Kumar said as he passed through the press of bewildered villagers. "I'm so glad to see people again. I can't tell you how lucky we are to be alive." Rajan stayed close beside him, his hand caressing his sword hilt, his eyes darting this way and that. Kumar put a reassuring arm around his shoulders. "It's all right, Rajan. We're safe now. These people will surely help us."

Rajan bit his lip and said nothing. A man dressed in a blue and white striped sweater and blue woolen trousers met them in the center near the fire pit. His black hair hung to his shoulders, and the people looked to him as if he were they're leader. He pulled off a pair of work-worn leather gloves and took Kumar's hand in a firm shake.

"Welcome to Bryne. My name is Agnar. I'm custodian of this village at the moment, though elections are not far off and my brother-in-law is making a bid for the job. I say all power to him, I have better things to do with my life than deal with everyone's petty squabbles." Agnar laughed.

Kumar gave him a grim smile. "Forgive me if I don't share your mirth until my son and I have had a drink of water. My name is Kumar Raza. This is my son, Rajan."

"Here, please," a woman with pale blond hair braided down past her waist pressed a cup of herbal tea into Kumar's hand. "Tis better than plain water and will set you feeling right in no time." She gave a similar cup to Rajan who took it, sank down beside the fire and swallowed an eager mouthful.

Kumar sipped the chamomile tea, letting the flavor wet his parched tongue and throat.

"Raza?" Agnar said. "The people of the mainland call you a great dragon hunter?"

"We're from Varna, actually. It's on the western side of the world. The city of Daro. In my younger days I was head of the dragon hunter jati there."

"I've never heard of that place. But we've never had contact with the west in my lifetime." Agnar smiled. "You must have hunted many dragons to get a name like that."

"Yes, though this hunt has not turned out exactly as I planned. We must truly be lost if you've never heard of Varna. That does not bode well for our return home."

"You just got here, and already so anxious to leave?" Agnar said good naturedly. "Here. Eat. Worry about getting home later. Be glad you're alive for now."

The woman had returned with two bowls of steaming stew. Kumar took the stew and sank down beside Rajan. "Thank you. I suppose we'll have to stay her for a few days. Is there a house where we can stay? I have a little money to pay room and board."

"This hall is free and open to all. If you decide to settle here, the villagers will work together to raise you a house. If not, you can buy passage to the mainland on the next ship that docks here. Though, in truth, they do not come here often. We have little to offer in the way of trade."

Kumar glanced at Rajan. His face was pale, and his hand shook as he tried to eat the stew. "I think perhaps we will stay here a few days only. We'll purchase some supplies from you, if we could, then head deeper into the island. Who knows what new dragons we could encounter? I mean, if we are stuck in this place, why not take advantage of it and ply our trade? Hunting dragons is what we do, after all. And my son . . . I'm afraid I raised him terribly. He's spent more time in the wild than in civilized places. He's quite shy around so many people."

Rajan shuddered and set his bowl down before his shaking hands dropped it.

Agnar stared down at Rajan for a moment. Frowned, then wiped the frown away with a smile. "That's it," he called to the crowd. "Our guests need peace and quiet and privacy. Go back home, back to work, what-have-you. Leave them in peace. Perhaps when they are recovered we will have a feast to celebrate their arrival."

On Agnar's orders, the crowd started to disperse, though many of them came up to shake Kumar's hand or slap him on the back in welcome before leaving the hall. Rajan kept his head down and refused to respond to anyone's greetings. Not the brother Kumar had known in their childhood. Once, Rajan would have been the first to call for a feast in celebration, and music and dancing. He would have greeted everyone with a smile and handshake and have learned all their names within moments of meeting them. Kumar swore at the red dragon under his breath and wished he had one more harpoon he could ram through its body.

## Chapter Five

**Rajan heaved a sigh** of relief when the last of the villagers left the hall. He rubbed his head. The press of their thoughts had nearly broken into his own. So many people. He shuddered. "I don't like this place, Kumar."

"We won't stay long."

"They were talking about building us a house so we could stay forever."

"We won't."

"I can't be around people. Their minds keep trying to push into mine." Rajan picked his stew bowl up and hurried to eat the rest. It was warm and tasted of dragonfish and vegetables. He devoured it greedily. For some reason it felt like it had been a long time since he'd had any decent food. Probably hadn't, locked up by the red dragon.

"You'll be all right. You can learn to shield your mind. You used to do it all the time."

"That was different back home in Daro. People's thoughts were more fuzzy then. I could only see into yours clearly. Now I've bonded with a dragon, it's like I have all this power tearing around in my head, and I don't know how to control it. I thought I'd be all right without Kanvar, but now I don't know. Let's leave first thing in the morning."

"All right." Kumar finished his own food. "I'll go buy the supplies now then." He grabbed the waterskins and walked out of the hall.

Rajan took a deep breath. He was alone now. Glad to be alone, just for a moment. He huddled close to the fire. The smell of burning pine seemed off. He was used to a different smell, sulfur from the red dragon's volcano. He tried to imagine what his life had been like there. Locked in a cage. The heat of the volcano heating the rocks beneath his feet. He rubbed his hand down his chest. He was scarred. Terribly scarred from burns on his chest, arms, and legs. He rubbed his face, feeling for scarring there. His cheeks were smooth of the mottled burn scars, but he felt one long slash across his right cheek. Beautiful, he thought. The ladies will really love that.

As if in response to his thought, a side door creaked open, and a young woman slipped into the hall. She hesitated when he looked over at her and put his hand on his sword hilt.

"What do you want?" He said. Then felt bad that his voice had come out so gruff. She was pretty with long blond hair, braided like the older woman who had given them food and drink. She wore a blue and red dress, a warm one with long sleeves, a high collar and, hem down to the floor. Her cheeks were rosy from the cold outside. Her face delicate.

She startled backward at the sound of his voice, then pulled herself together and smiled. "My name is Gerda. I noticed your grandfather had left and thought you might like some company." She crossed the hall and sat down close beside him.

"I don't need company."

"But surely you'd like some."

Rajan shook his head. "I like to be alone."

She let out a crystal laugh and rested her hand on his leg. "No one wants to be alone."

Rajan jumped to his feet and moved away. "Gerda, please, you don't understand." He fiddled with his hands, unsure where to put them. On his sword hilt felt the most natural, but that couldn't be the right place for dealing with a woman.

"No, it's you who doesn't understand. Do you know how many single girls there are in this village?"

"Uh, no." Rajan strode around to the far side of the fire. Her face did look beautiful with the light from the flames reflecting off it.

"Fifteen."

"All right."

"Want to guess how many young men, even counting the ugly ones?"

Rajan shook his head. "My grandfather and I are just passing through. We're leaving in the morning."

"Five." Gerda walked around the fire, dainty steps, swaying hips.

Rajan shook his head again, trying to clear it from her thoughts that ignited in his mind. She was lonely. Desperate. He was handsome, despite the scar on his cheek.

"Surely there are other villages." He measured her stride, going in the opposite direction, keeping the fire pit between them.

"Boats from other places only come here once or twice a year. You're stuck on this island for at least that long. What's wrong, don't you think I'm pretty enough?"

Rajan swallowed. "You're pretty. But I am a . . . not a nice man. You'd be better off alone your whole life than with me." He couldn't tell her he was a Naga. Yet she was pressing him.

"Rajan, that's a nice name. I bet you are a nice man, despite what you say."

Rajan bolted for the main door, but she caught his arm before he reached it. Her fingers, soft and warm, held him.

"Rajan, please wait." She swung around in front of him and pressed her torso up against his chest. Her free hand went to his face, stroking his cheek. "Kiss me."

"No." Heat spread through his body. Would it be so bad? One kiss? She was beautiful.

She wrapped her hand around the back of his head and pulled it down toward her. He only half resisted, her lips looked warm and inviting. They touched his, gentle, sweet. And her mind exploded into his. Her mother, yelling at her to sweep the kitchen. Her father repairing his fishing boat. The scent of chamber pots she emptied. The fight she'd had that morning with her sister. Her wants, her needs, her yearning. The fire she felt as she kissed him.

The sudden overwhelming thoughts startled him, and he pushed her away. "Leave me alone." The words left his lips, accompanied by a rush of power, pushing her mind out of his own.

Gerda gasped, and her eyes went blank. She took a step back and stood there, staring at nothing. Saying nothing.

Rajan waited for her to yell at him, slap him, do anything in response. None came.

"Gerda?" he said.

She didn't respond.

He reached a hand out to her.

Her eyes remained blank as if she were deaf and blind.

"Gerda?" He touched her forehead, looking for her thoughts and found nothing. Her mind was blank. His power had blown it away like dandelion fluff in a hurricane.

Rajan's mouth went dry. A tingle spread through his hands up, his arms, and a pain of regret blossomed in his chest for what he'd done. He'd destroyed her. Worse than killed her. "What kind of a monster am I?" he whispered.

Then it struck him. When the villagers found Gerda like this, they'd know he was a Naga. They'd know, and they'd kill him and Kumar too.

Swearing, he grabbed Kumar's supply pack, slung it onto his back—it was heavy, how had his brother hefted it around so easily—and ran from the hall. He sent his thoughts searching for Kumar the moment his feet hit the wooden walkway outside. He sensed his brother at a shop down and over a few houses. His feet carried him there, with fear chasing after him.

Kumar had the filled waterskins over his shoulder and had just paid for a load of supplies and tucked them under his arm when Rajan burst through the door.

"We have to go," Rajan said, grabbing him and dragging him out. "Now, right now."

Kumar resisted and slipped out of his grasp.

Rajan did not wait to argue. He sprinted toward the docks and jumped into the boat. Kumar didn't catch him until he'd already untied it from the dock and was starting to push off into the bay.

"Rajan, wait." Kumar tossed the supplies into the boat and leaped in after him. "What's the hurry?"

"Tell you later." Rajan got one of the oars and started rowing while calling Silverwave to come get them.

"Hey wait," someone called from the dock behind.

Kumar picked up the other oar and looked back. It was Agnar. "Sorry Agnar, looks like my son sighted a rare dragon and wants to go after it now. I'll be back for the rest of the supplies later." He dug the oar in and helped pull the boat out of the bay. As soon as they were far enough away the villagers wouldn't see, Silverwave surface and took the harness with the rope attached to the boat that Rajan tossed her.

Rajan set the oar down and buried his face in his hands. The air he breathed into his lunges felt like a furnace, hot with shame.

Kumar sat on the bench across from him. Rajan sensed his eyes resting on him and the questions in his mind. But Kumar remained silent, waiting for him to speak and explain their sudden exit from the village.

A tremor of self loathing went through Rajan. He jumped to his feet and tried to go over the side of the boat, but Kumar grabbed him and forced him back down to the bench with a strength that startled Rajan.

"No. Don't get wet again. It's too cold. Just sit down and tell me what's wrong."

Rajan tried to speak, but his throat knotted up and no words came out.

"Rajan," Kumar's stern tone demanded an explanation.

Rajan tried once more to admit what he'd done, but horror of it turned his stomach and he leaned over the edge of the boat, retching in bitter pain instead.

He felt concern flare through his brother's mind.

"You didn't . . . kill someone, did you?" Kumar said.

That sent another tremor through Rajan's body. The fact that his brother thought he would, thought he could, murder one of the villagers sent terror through him. What am I? he wondered. What have I done? The black wall in his mind taunted him. Most of his life was hidden behind it. Judging by the gray in Kumar's hair, Rajan had been bound to the red dragon for the time it takes for a boy to become a man and grow into old age.

"Rajan." Kumar's voice was softer this time. He moved onto the bench beside him and rested a hand on his back. "Relax. Breathe."

Rajan tore away from him and moved to the far side of the boat. "You think I killed someone? Why? Why would I?"

*Perhaps you were hungry*, Kumar thought, then caught himself and tried to build a shield around his mind, hoping Rajan hadn't heard it.

"Hungry?" Rajan shrieked. He was shaking now and couldn't stop. Sweat streamed down the back of his neck though the ocean wind chilled him.

*Red dragons eat humans*, Silverwave said into his mind. She meant her thoughts to soothe and calm him.

*Did I? Are you saying I did?*

Silverwave's memories seeped into his mind. Kanvar had not erased or imprisoned those. Silverwave lay curled in a corner of a filthy cavern. She watched the Great Red dragon drag a human man out of a cage and over to a blood-spattered pit where Rajan waited. He had steel claws strapped to his hands. The man screamed as the dragon thrust him into the pit. Only Rajan climbed back out.

Rajan sucked in a breath and drew his sword. *How many people did I kill, did I eat?* The memory of the taste of blood clung to his mouth and no amount of swallowing could dilute it.

*I do not know.* Silverwave's thoughts were a river of sorrow. *But, Rajan, it wasn't you. It was the red dragon. He controlled your mind and body. There was nothing of you left. You were merely a weapon in his hands. One cannot blame a sword for slaughtering people. It is the wielder of the sword who is responsible.*

*Okay, then, don't blame the sword for this.* Rajan twisted his sword horizontally and slashed it toward his own neck.

Kumar caught his wrist just as the sword made contact with his skin, stopping the strike. The crushing pain of Kumar's grip forced Rajan's hand open, and the sword thudded to the bottom of the boat.

"Let me go," Rajan cried. "Let me die!"

"No." Kumar slammed him down onto the bench and held him there while he grabbed a vial of dragon saliva from his pack.

Rajan's neck stung as Kumar rubbed the saliva across the cut.

Rajan struggled to get away, but Kumar kept him pinned until the wound healed over. Then he released him with an angry grunt. "Try that again and I'll thrash your backside."

Rajan rolled away to kneel on the bottom of the boat. The sword hilt rested against his knee. He reached for it, but Kumar grabbed his wrist again in that crushing grip.

"Rajan, do not make me tie you up. Just sit still and tell me what happened in the village." Kumar grabbed the sword and moved it out of Rajan's reach.

Rajan slumped down to lie on the floor of the boat and rested his head against the wooden planks. All strength left his body. His stomach twisted and heaved like the ocean waves that kept them afloat. He wondered where Kanvar was, how Kanvar could have left him to deal with this alone. He said it was better that they face it together, but then he probably thought the memories would stay locked away until Kumar and Rajan reached Kundiland. He'd forgotten about Silverwave, or had not known how detailed her own memories were.

"I didn't kill anyone . . . in the village," Rajan croaked. "There was a girl. She tried to kiss me. I pushed her away. Told her to leave me alone. My words, three simple words, destroyed her mind. Wiped it blank. I don't know how. I didn't mean for it to happen."

Kumar raked his fingers through his beard. "You wiped her mind?"

Rajan nodded. At least he hadn't tried to eat her. He glanced up at the incriminating bite scar on Kumar's face.

"Ah, well. She'll probably recover."

"I don't think so." The bitter taste of blood and bile clung to his mouth.

"Well, Brother, as someone who's been on the receiving end of that sort of thing, I can tell you from my own experience, her mind will resolve itself in time. Mine did. Of course it took over twelve years, but I did recover." Kumar leaned back against the bench and spread his legs out on the bottom of the boat, so he sat beside where Rajan lay.

"Someone wiped your mind?" Kumar had sparked Rajan's curiosity.

"Amar. The Naga king."

"You said you were friends."

"We were. Best friends, but he startled me one day, and I startled him, and he reacted without thinking." Kumar laughed. "He didn't mean to do it. It was pure reflex, and believe me if Amar who has had five hundred years of training to use his powers only for good can reflexively blow his best friend's mind away, it's not surprising that you who have only been bound to the silver dragon for a short time should make a similar mistake."

"But the girl."

"She'll recover. And it's my fault anyway, isn't it? I forced you to go to the village when you didn't want to. I was selfish. The fault is mine, not yours, and I'm sorry."

Rajan rocked his head back and forth against the wooden floor of the boat. "But I *did* eat people."

Kumar grunted. "We can't know that for sure."

"I killed them and ate them, when I was bound to the red dragon. Silverwave watched me do it."

"What?" Kumar sat upright.

"You forgot to tell Kanvar to erase Silverwave's memories as well." Rajan squeezed his eyes closed and curled into a ball.

Kumar started swearing and didn't stop for a long, long time.

## Chapter Six

**Kanvar stood on the** crest of a hill overlooking a farm valley dotted with fields and cottages. "There are so many people on this continent, Bensharie. Who would have guessed?" The afternoon sun was warm on his face, and the breeze carried the scent of roasted itchekin.

*I don't think anyone saw us.* Bensharie dug his claws into the soft grass and spread his wings. Kanvar rolled his shoulders, feeling how stiff and sore Bensharie had grown during their days of flying. He wasn't bound to Bensharie, but the mental link between the two of them had deepened, and they felt comfortable sharing more than just speech now.

"I'm pretty sure that farmer back there noticed the ripple as we passed overhead. He stared straight at us, but he didn't seem surprised or worried. Do you suppose there are other gold dragons on this continent, and they get along with the humans?"

*Maybe.* Bensharie curled up to get some rest.

Kanvar frowned and checked to make sure his crossbow and bolts were secure. In the back of his mind, Dharanidhar's stomach rumbled with hunger. Kanvar still could not believe that Rajahansa had banished him, but then the two dragons had always been enemies. Still, Dhar had not been as successful in hunting blind as Kanvar would have liked. He knew he had to get back to Dharanidhar soon. But Bensharie needed to rest before they could fly on. "I'm going to find us something to eat." Maybe if he filled his own belly it would help Dharanidhar not be so hungry.

*Go buy something from the farmer. That itchekin smells good.* Bensharie licked his lips. *And get some water from his well while you're at it.*

"Right." Kanvar limped down the hill. The way was smooth and grassy and did not give him too much trouble. He stepped onto the road and headed for the farmhouse at the base of the hill, but the farmer met him just beyond the short rock wall that marked the boundary of his fields. He was dressed in gray homespun clothes. A straw hat shielded his face from the sun. The mud on the hem of his trousers and on the shovel he carried over his shoulder indicated he'd stopped his labors to come out and meet Kanvar.

"Nice day for a flight," the farmer said, glancing up to the top of the hill where Bensharie lay then fixing his eyes on Kanvar.

Kanvar cleared his throat and tensed. If the farmer had seen him flying with the dragon he'd know Kanvar was a Naga. Who knew what he'd do.

"Long walk down the hill," the farmer said. "You could have just landed in the road like everyone else. I do have my tribute ready for you, and I've never been behind on my payments."

Kanvar sucked in a surprised breath and tried to process what the farmer had said. Could it be that there were still places in the world where the Nagas ruled?

"I, um. Bensharie didn't want to startle your bov-inders." Kanvar waved toward the domestic lesser dragons that grazed in the field behind the stone farmhouse.

"That's thoughtful of him." The farmer shifted his shovel from one shoulder to the other. "Well, come on in and I'll get the tribute for you."

"Actually," Kanvar stayed rooted to the spot in the road. "I'm not here for tribute. I just stopped to refill my waterskin and buy some food."

The farmer dropped the head of the shovel to the ground and leaned on the handle, looking Kanvar over before speaking again. "You're a youngun ain't you? I didn't think they let the children fly out this far alone."

"Please, I can pay for the food and water." The farmer's words meant there was more than one Naga somewhere—mothers and fathers and children? Unbelievable. The thought made Kanvar jittery.

The farmer scratched his chin. "You running away?"

"No. I'm trying to get back home."

"Come to think of it. I ain't never seen a crippled Naga before. I thought they killed all the deformed ones at birth."

"Right. Never mind." Kanvar started back up the hill.

The farmer waited a moment before striding to catch up to him. He made no move to stop Kanvar, just walked along beside him. "Your mother must have loved you dearly to keep you hidden from His Lordship."

Kanvar pressed his lips together and refused to answer. *Bensharie*, he called. *I think you better come get me.* Sunshine rippled at the top of the hill as Bensharie stood and took to the air.

"You don't have to fly off," the farmer said. "I would not dare lay a hand on any Naga, crippled or no. What do I know about it anyway? Maybe there's a dozen crippled Nagas. All I hear out here are rumors. Come back to the house. I'll give you food and water. Milk from the bovinders if you want. That waterskin's not going to carry enough water to slake your dragon's thirst. Since he's on his way down, I'll fill a water trough for him."

Kanvar stopped and pivoted to face the farmer. "Why are you being nice to me?"

The farmer's brow wrinkled. "Why wouldn't I be?"

"If the Nagas rule over these lands and force you to pay tribute, shouldn't you hate them? Don't you want to be free of their abusive rule?" The opposite side of the world seemed to be all backwards and inside out.

"I've never known any Naga to be abusive."

"How could you tell if they were? They'd simply take control of your mind and make you think they aren't. Doesn't that worry you, the fact that they can read your thoughts and control your emotions?" Sweat slicked Kanvar's hands and he reached for his crossbow. It made him feel better just checking to be sure it was there.

The farmer chuckled. "Something of a little rebel aren't you?"

Bensharie's wings kicked sand up from the road as he flapped to a landing beside Kanvar.

"Greetings." The farmer bowed to Bensharie. "Bring your Naga friend and come back to the house. My wife's been dead two years now, and my sons have gone off to work in the city, but I'd be happy to prepare some supper for you both." The farmer strode back toward the house, leaving Kanvar and Bensharie alone on the road.

*His Lordship?* Bensharie said. *Sounds ominous. How many Nagas do you suppose there are?*

"I don't know." Kanvar rubbed his sweaty hand on his leg. "And I don't want to know, not right now anyway. I have to get back and help Dharanidhar."

*What if there were enough Nagas and dragons to help your father fight General Chandran and his armies?*

Kanvar jerked in surprise. "My father doesn't want to fight them. We don't want a war, Bensharie. People will get hurt. Killed. You don't want that, do you?"

*No, but I don't want to see my family slaughtered either.*

Kanvar bit his lip. The farmer had gone around to the well and was filling a water trough beside it. "Bensharie, if the Nagas aren't hated and hunted here, maybe we could bring your family and mine to live here. We'd be safe. Everything would be all right."

*Ignoring the His Lordship killing the crippled babies bit?*

Kanvar frowned.

The farmer finished filling the trough and went inside the house.

*And the I have your tribute ready for you bit?*

"Bensharie, please."

*I don't like that your father and mine have been arguing.* Bensharie rippled his wings and scratched at the road with his claws. *Maybe I should have stayed with writing poetry. Heroes and battles and conflict look better as ink on paper than in real life.*

"I agree."

The two of them stood in silence for a moment.

*That roasted itchekin does smell good.*

"Right." Kanvar rubbed Bensharie's shoulder, and the two of them made their way to the farmhouse and supper.

**Raahi left his little** brother, Tiago, breaking open geodes behind the house and sprinted up the mountainside. He had strapped two new spears to his back, spears with steel heads he had crafted himself and was anxious to try out.

The bushes and twisted trees that grew up the side of the mountain smelled of the sweet rain that had fallen the night before. The muddy ground was springy beneath his feet. A scaly ibex bleated from the rocks above. Raahi would love to bag an ibex someday. He'd tried a half dozen times since he got home without success. The ibex were too large and agile for him to take down easily. And they could fly as well as leap over his head. Perhaps if Raahi had a crossbow like Kumar Raza. Well, Raahi supposed Kumar Raza could probably bring down an ibex with a kitchen knife, but that was beside the point. Today, Raahi wasn't hunting ibex. His father needed some gray dragon hide to finish off the handles on some swords he'd fashioned.

The lesser gray dragons were more Raahi's size. They had wings, but could only jump and glide so far. They hunted the kitrats and other vermin in the mornings. Then, in the afternoon, bellies full, would crawl out to sun themselves on the cliffs in the afternoon. Tired and full, the gray dragons became sluggish and complacent. Raahi had become quite good at spearing them in this state.

He slowed and pulled a spear from his harness as he reached the base of the cliffs. Ignoring his racing heart,

Raahi licked his lips and crept over to the rocks. The gray dragons blended in with the shale cliff, and it took Raahi a moment to spot a group of six sunning themselves within reach. Silence was his friend now. He eased into range and slammed the spear forward. It surprised the gray dragon, jabbing through its chest and pinning it to the rock. The rest of the dragons in the bunch scattered.

Delighted, Raahi pulled his catch free and held it up to examine. Very nice. His father would be pleased.

A shadow passed over him. He looked up into the sunlight sky, but could see nothing. Be careful, Raahi reminded himself. There were some dragons on the mountain big enough to eat him for dinner. The ibex wouldn't attack. They ate plants not meat, but a good-sized mountain drake could be deadly. The smell of the dead gray dragon might attract a drake if it were close by. Raahi pulled his spear free and scanned the sky for any sign of a mountain drake.

"Good afternoon, Raahi."

The voice startled Raahi. He spun around and saw Kanvar's brother step out of the trees. "Devaj?" Raahi said, suprised. "Was that your dragon overhead?"

An amused smile creased Devaj's face. "Yes, I suppose it was."

"What brings you to Darvat? Karishi went home with you. I've been hoping Kanvar would come for a visit." Just like the last time Devaj had visited, Raahi felt comfortable in his presence. He knew Devaj was a Naga, a prince, but Devaj was so much less intimidating than Karishi, or even Kanvar. Like he was Raahi's big brother too or something. A feeling of peace settled over Raahi.

"I'm sorry Kanvar couldn't come," Devaj said. "His dragon has still not recovered. In fact, that's why I'm here. I'm very worried about my little brother."

"He's hurt that badly?" Raahi set the dead gray dragon down and leaned his spear against it. "What can I do to help?"

Devaj's smile widened. "I knew I could count on you. Come sit with me a minute and let's talk. I have much to tell you."

Devaj found a boulder and sat comfortably on the ground with his back against it. Raahi followed him over, anxious to learn how he could help Devaj and Kanvar.

**A vast shoreline filled** the horizon from one side to the other. "I guess that's the continent," Rajan said. "Looks like your map is accurate." He rubbed away the red marks on his wrists where Kumar's ropes had bound him. Twice Kumar had fallen asleep, and twice more Rajan tried to kill himself until Kumar had taken to tying his hands together before closing his eyes to rest. Now Kumar was awake and the ropes came off. Rajan knew it was useless to try anything. Silverwave slept while Kumar was awake, and Kumar slept while Silverwave pulled them. He was doomed to stay alive and live with himself, though the bloody images from Silverwave's memories haunted him.

"It's a good thing. We're about out of water and food again. I wish I'd had a bit more time to restock on that island." Kumar put everything back in his pack and cinched it up. It seemed he was ready for anything like a good dragon hunter should be.

Rajan recalled the lessons he'd learned back at the dragon hunter complex in Daro. Old Qadim, their advanced hunt teacher, slapping the wooden desk with his whip yelling at them, "Never go on a hunt alone, never go unprepared." The dust flying up to form shimmering sparkles in the ray of sunlight from the window. That life was now lost to Rajan forever. He felt an emptiness in his chest. All he wanted was to be a dragon hunter. The best dragon hunter that ever lived. But Kumar had accomplished that without him—Kumar Raza, the Great Dragon Hunter—with a crazy brother he had to tie up just to keep him alive.

Rajan watched the shore fill the horizon. Frothy waves crashed and thundered against towering rocks. There was no place to put ashore as far as he could see.

*Ask Kumar which way we should go*, Silverwave said. *North along the coast, or south?*

Rajan gritted his teeth. He did not want to talk to his brother. "North or south?" Rajan asked. "I'd prefer south. I'm tired of the cold."

"North," Kumar Raza answered. "It would take us forever to follow the southern shore around."

Rajan groaned and relayed Kumar's decision.

Silverwave obliged, changing direction so their little life boat skimmed over the waves parallel to the dangerous shore.

"Are your wrists all right?" Kumar asked.

Rajan turned his back on his brother and trailed his fingers over the edge of the boat in the water. It felt like the whole of the ocean that swept along Silverwave's sides as she swam. He wished he could go below with her, breathe in the depths, live with the fish, never have to speak to another human again.

"Tell Silverwave to look for fresh water. These cliffs can't go on forever. There has to be an inlet somewhere." Kumar's gruff voice made Rajan wince. He wondered if his own voice would sound like that when he'd grown old.

"She knows what she's doing."

Kumar grunted in acknowledgment and they both fell silent, not speaking to each other again until hours later when Silverwave pulled the lifeboat into a quiet cove and hauled it up onto a golden beach.

Kumar leaped out of the boat, grabbed the waterskins, and made directly for the bank of a little river that fed into the cove.

Rajan stepped out of the boat and stretched. Silverwave wrapped her coils around him and rested her head on his chest, blinking up at him with silver eyes. He stroked the scar on her cheek. *Why did you save me*, he asked her.

*Because I didn't like what the red dragon had done to you. Because you look like Kumar, and Kumar is my friend. He rescued me from whalers. Because everyone deserves another chance at life. Because I could.*

Rajan grimaced.

*I wish you would cease trying to throw our lives away. You may hate yourself, but I don't hate you, and I'm not ready to die yet.*

*I'm sorry, Silverwave.* Rajan sank to the sand and pulled his knees up to his chest. *I just don't want to accidentally hurt anyone else, especially not my brother. Do you suppose he realizes I could take over his mind and force him to untie me anytime I want? I could destroy his memories in a flash second just like I did Gerda's. I could command his heart to stop beating, and it would. Does he know that, Silver? He should. If he had any sense he would leave me here and run as far and as fast as he can to get away from me.*

*Perhaps he feels you will not harm him. You are his brother.*

Rajan watched Kumar fill the waterskins and then trek back to the lifeboat and hand one to Rajan. Rajan took it reluctantly.

"I'm going to hunt us some dinner. No villages here. No people to make your life difficult."

"Only you." Rajan took a gulp of water then capped the waterskin and tossed it into the boat.

Kumar frowned. "Silverwave, don't let him do anything stupid while I'm gone." He strode away and followed the river upstream without looking back.

Rajan got to his feet. Found where Kumar had stashed the sword in the boat, and shoved it into the sheath at his waist. "He thinks he's so good, like he's the only one who can hunt for dinner. I'll show him."

Silverwave tightened her coils around Rajan, holding him in place. *I must stay with you and I need to stay near the water.*

"Let me go. I'm not going to do anything. I'm just going hunting. I think there may be some lesser black serpents in the water upstream."

*Promise me you will not harm yourself.*

Rajan fingered his sword hilt and thought for a moment what it would be like to chop off Silverwave's head. They would both die. She couldn't stop him then, could she. Her coils rippled in agitation.

"Silver," he said aloud. "I have to kill something. So is it going to be you and me or a lesser serpent? You decide."

Silverwave hissed, pulled away from him, and launching herself across the sand into the cove.

Rajan huffed and made his way across the stream into the underbrush. Leafy trees grew thick in the ravine that the stream ran through. He could hear Kumar moving ahead on the far side, making his way up the ravine to the wider forest above the cove. Rajan swung at the bushes with his sword. It felt good to be cutting, slashing, destroying, taking his anger and frustration out on the vines and sticks. The weight of the sword pressed into his palm, the resistance of the plants he hacked let his arm muscles feel the fire of his movement. He came against a broad tree trunk that blocked his path along the riverbank.

"I hate you." He yelled, chopping at the tree trunk. Bark exploded beneath each of his strokes, stinging his arms and face. "I hate you. I hate you." If only the tree trunk could be the red dragon's neck. If only the sword could chop through burning red scales. If only it could chop away all the lost years. It could chop back the crossbow bolt his uncle had shot him with, chop away the dragon fever that had taken him.

He kept swinging at the tree until his arms grew too tired to lift the sword for another blow. Then he dropped the sword and fell to his knees. "I hate you!" he screamed to the whole world.

Kumar cleared his throat behind him, and Rajan looked over his shoulder at his brother who stood on the bank with a pair of green lesser serpents in his hands.

"Good work, Rajan," Kumar said. "I think that tree is quite dead now, and you scared these beauties up from the brush so I could take them. Let's go eat." He headed back to the cove.

Rajan dragged himself to his feet and forced his burning arms to pick up the sword and sheath it. The edge was dulled from its battering against the tree. He'd have to sharpen it before bed if he wanted to make use of it again.

He made no effort to walk quickly back to the boat, lingering instead in the shade beneath the trees, listening to the babble of the water. He was spent, too numb now to feel any emotion at all. By the time he reached the boat, Kumar had already started a fire and finished skinning the serpents.

## Chapter Seven

**Bensharie landed on the** eastern coast of the continent just before sunset. It had taken them three days to fly across the vast expanse. Kanvar had been jittery ever since their encounter with the farmer. Part of him wanted to meet the Nagas of this land, but part of him feared them. Even his own father's dragon had rejected him as an abomination because of his deformities. Whoever His Lordship was, or any of his followers, were likely to strike Kanvar down on sight. Better to stay unseen. Stay away from the farmlands and the villages. Stick to the ridges of a mountain chain that crossed the expanse. No more trying to buy food.

Since Bensharie wasn't a hunter, Kanvar had hunted for their meals. They had not gone hungry, though Dharanidhar had. Perhaps the seals smelled the dragon in the cove and that was why they stayed away or perhaps they heard Dhar coming as he lumbered out of Akshara's lair, either way he'd only gotten a few of them since Amar had left him there alone.

*How far do you suppose it is from here to Kundiland?* Bensharie said. *If it takes more than a day, I'm not sure I can make it. I'm not as big as Dharanidhar and your weight is heavy for me.*

Kanvar looked out across the open blue sky and down over the rolling waves. "If we need to rest, you can land in the water and I'll swim until you get your breath back. I don't see any sign of a storm like the one that nearly killed Dharanidhar. Our biggest problem could be food and fresh water if it takes us too long to cross."

*That's not reassuring me.*

"We have no choice but to try, Bensharie. We can't stay here and let Dharanidhar starve to death."

Bensharie growled in agreement. They spent the evening gathering food and water. In the morning, they took off into a bright sunrise.

**Rajan squinted into the** sunrise, trying to get a better view of the shoreline. For the past two days they'd been hard pressed to find a spit of beach not inhabited by some fishing village or larger town. So much of the coast was rocky and inaccessible that anywhere it smoothed out, every cove and bay, people had settled in. He and Kumar had done their best to stay away from people and had succeeded so far, but now human contact seemed impossible to avoid. The towering cliffs had fallen away to level land, and a city bigger than Daro filled the space between the thick forests and the bay.

Big three-masted sail boats and small fishing boats dotted the water. The overwhelming press of people's thoughts crashed against Rajan's mind like breakers against the cliffs.

"I don't like this," Rajan said.

Kumar Raza frowned. "I don't either. But we're out of food and water. We have to restock."

Rajan gripped the side of the boat and refused to return the friendly wave of a fisherman who sailed past them. Silverwave dove beneath the surface to remain unseen until the man had gone by.

As the sun rose higher, the city came more into view. On the west side, along the shore of a wide river, stood tall white mansions with regal pillars and arches glittering in the sunlight. Lawns and gardens separated the mansions. Wide flagstone streets led from one to another. Largest of all, a palace built from the same white limestone rose up beside the river. Its walls threw everything around it in shadow. Towers rose above the ramparts. Golden flags with a white fountain in the center flapped in the wind.

"It's almost as big as the palace at Stonefountain," Kumar muttered. "Look at those arched windows in the tower. Humans have no need for windows that large. And those flags bear the Stonefountain crest."

"What are you saying?" Rajan's eyes followed the wide streets down into the rest of the city where the mansions gave way to smaller stone houses followed by wooden ones and then narrow streets crowded with rickety shacks and hovels made of mud and hanging rugs.

Kumar scanned the skies. "I don't see any Great Gold dragons. Not in flight anyway, and if they're holding still I won't see them at all, but, Rajan, I've been to Stonefountain, and ignoring the lack of a central mountain and the placement of river to one side instead of the center, this city is laid out like the one at Stonefountain."

Rajan sat back on the bench and fingered his sword hilt. "You think Nagas built it?"

"We know they flew around the world. We know that island we stopped on was an outpost. If you discovered a land as fair as this one, would you not settle it?" Kumar ran his fingers through his beard and shifted uncomfortably on the bench. "The question is, did the Nagas here meet the same fate as those at Stonefountain?"

Rajan rubbed his head. With the press of tens of thousands of people against his mind, he'd never be able to tell if one or two were Nagas. "I don't know, but we can't stop here. I will go insane if we try. I'll tell Silverwave to get us past as quickly as possible, as best she can without being seen by so many other boats. I'm not sure I even care if she's seen. I want out of here now. We'll stop for supplies on the coast as soon as we've left the city behind."

"But if there are Nagas, maybe they can help you learn to control your powers." Kumar grabbed an oar and started paddling toward shore.

*"No,"* Rajan said, and used his power to back up his command. "Not after what happened the last time I got around people."

Kumar stopped rowing and stared at him. "You're using your power to control me? Your brother?"

"Yes. Whatever it takes. We are not going ashore here. I don't want to meet any other Nagas. We don't even know if there are any. As far as we know, these people hate Nagas as much as everyone else."

"But the flags. They wouldn't be flying the Stone-fountain flags if—"

"I said, no." *Silverwave, get us out of here.*

Silverwave broke the surface and shook her head and neck sending water droplets flying. *Something's wrong, Rajan. Something feels wrong with the ocean. It's tense. The fish are frightened.*

*All the more reason to get out of here as quickly as possible.*

Silverwave agreed with him. She slipped back into the harness and started pulling the lifeboat past all the other boats on the water. But she grew more and more tense each passing moment. *The water is stretching. The ocean floor is moving.* She stopped swimming and spread her wing fins, fanning them in the water.

A cry went up from one of the nearby fishing boats, and a man pointed toward shore. Rajan snapped his gaze in that direction and saw the buildings had started to sway.

"It's an earthquake!" Kumar shouted. "Silverwave, get us out to sea. As far and fast as you can. Get us out of here!"

Silverwave shook her terror away and started swimming away from shore. Rajan stared at the rocking buildings, unable to tear his eyes away as the mud hovels and stick huts began to collapse, followed in a rippling wave across the city by bigger and bigger houses.

*Rajan.* Silverwave's urgent cry finally made him look away from shore. He realized that the water below their boat had sucked away, becoming shallow enough he could see the ocean floor beneath them.

Kumar swore. "Keep swimming Silverwave. Straight away from land as fast as you can."

Silverwave thrashed in the shallow water, dragging the boat behind her. Rajan gripped the side and glanced out to sea and then back at the shaking city behind them then back out to sea. The horizon vanished behind a rising wall of water. The giant wave sucked in all the water around it and grew bigger and bigger, blocking the way to the open ocean. It towered in front of them like a mountain, a living, moving mountain—water flashing in the sunlight and then blocking out the sunlight, shadowing darkness, smelling of salt and sea and the darkest depths.

*What do I do?* Silverwave cried. It was clear that even at her fastest speed she would not be able to pull them over the top of that wave before it came crashing down, and if she stayed tethered to the boat she would meet its fate.

*Swim!* Rajan yelled. *Dive for the base and head under it.*

*I can't pull you under it.*

*Yes you can. Trust me, this will work. Swim, Silverwave.*

Silverwave redoubled her efforts. Rajan drew his sword, leaped to the front of the boat, and sliced the blade through the rope that connected Silverwave to them.

Good thing I sharpened that, he thought as the line snapped and Silverwave flashed forward, disappearing into the rising tidal wave. He sheathed the sword and turned to face Kumar as the monstrous bulk of the ocean rose above them. "Well, at least she'll make it out of this alive."

"Not if you don't." Kumar tore one of the wooden benches from the boat and thrust it into Rajan's hands. "Hold your breath. Trust the air in your lungs to buoy you to the surface. Use the bench to stay afloat. Stay calm." Kumar grabbed him in a hug, then the ocean crashed down on top of them, tearing them apart. The boat flipped up and smacked Rajan in the back of the head before tumbling away. His eyesight went dark. The press of water crushed him. He screamed with his mind, and his thoughts were joined by thousands of other people screaming too.

# Chapter Eight

*We are dragon. We were burning, but the flame has been snuffed out. Water everywhere surrounds us. We can't breathe. We need heat. We need fire. Salt water drowns our tongue. We are screaming, but no sound comes out. There is thunder all around as we are slammed against the ground by a great wave and rolled over and over like a pebble on the beach, colliding with wood and stone and other people all caught up in one horrifying nightmare.*

**The water threw Rajan down** one last time and washed away from him. He rolled onto his hands and knees and coughed until he could draw air back into his lungs. His battered body throbbed with pain, foremost, the sharp stab from the back of his head where the lifeboat had hit it and shattered the wall that had once been there, locking up his memories.

He reared back onto his hind legs and roared as the memories flooded into his mind. He was dragon, fire and fury, and had almost succeeded in conquering the human lands. The helpless humans were at his mercy and then . . . one crippled serving boy had stopped him with the power of a singing stone so vast it could only be that greatest of stones clawed from Stonefountain by Akshara himself.

Kanvar, the crippled Naga, had subdued the Great Red dragon's power and handed Rajan over to the Maranies for execution. Rage filled him and he clawed at the refuse of sticks and stones and cloth left around him by the wave as it crashed ashore and washed back out to sea. But the rocks and wood broke his nails and scraped his skin, leaving him bleeding. He was not his dragon self. He was his human self. His dragon self had sent him to take control of the humans in this soft vulnerable body.

Growling, Rajan stared down at his bloody, shaking hands. His claws were gone. His wings were gone. He was not dragon now. He was . . . a man.

"Kanvar!" He screamed. Kanvar had trapped him in this body. The Maranies had tried to execute him but . . . Kanvar again. Kanvar had saved him. Taken him to a boat, to a man who looked like his father but wasn't. They had bound him and left the singing stone on him. Such agony. Akshara's stone, cutting him off from his dragon self. Isolating him in terrible pain, alone. Worse, they had done worse. The memories like the tidal waved crashed through his mind. And that little silver wyrm had helped them. Shown them the way to his dragon self's lair.

Rajan tore off his shirt and stared down at the four inch scar on his chest above his heart. Kanvar and his gold dragon and the man who looked like Rajan's father but wasn't had killed his dragon self. The singing stone had blocked him from seeing through his dragon self's eyes, but he had felt the pain of their strikes, the greater half of himself tear away in death, and the silver serpent forcing her own blood into his mouth, forcing her mind into his own, her soul into him, becoming his other half as if she could ever equal the greatness of his red dragon self. He searched for her with his mind, but could not feel her now.

Whining, Rajan pawed his head. These four enemies had killed him and forced him to live again. They'd destroyed his power and left him weak. They'd doused his fire and frozen him in the depths of the ocean. He hated them. And he hated himself. He curled into a ball amid the wreckage of the city, growling and moaning and wishing for the heat of the volcano to warm him.

But the red heat never came. Gradually he stilled and fell silent, becoming aware of other noises around him. A vast city destroyed by the ocean's anger. Moans and cries for help filled the air. He felt the presence of the hurt and frightened humans brush up against his mind. Humans were always hurt and frightened. He knew that well, had lived with it so long in the dragon's lair with the humans locked in their cages. He knew how to block out their thoughts . . . to silence them when he grew annoyed enough. But his red dragon self did not like him to kill more than they could eat in a day. He liked the meat fresh, and warm blood on his tongue.

Rajan licked his lips. He was hungry and there were plenty of humans, living and newly dead, around him. He climbed to his feet, unsteady for a moment just on two feet. Why were humans, of all creatures, stuck with only two feet? So irritating, especially when the ground was strewn with wreckage.

He kicked a board aside. It looked familiar, a seat from the lifeboat that had carried him to his doom. Someone had shoved it into his arms to give him a chance to survive the great wave that overshadowed him. The man that looked like his father but wasn't. The man who said he was his brother. . . . His brother.

Rajan choked. Kumar? His brother. His twin. His other self before his red dragon self had found him.

"Kumar?" He turned, scanning the fallen houses. He stood in a part of the city where the houses had been hovels of sticks and mud. Everything was leveled by the earthquake and then flung in disarray by the wave. There were bodies everywhere, alive and dead. None of them looked like his father. None like his brother grown old. He felt for Kumar's mind, but found nothing. "Kumar?"

He blinked. Kumar Raza was his enemy. He had killed his dragon self. Was he enemy or brother? And Kanvar had trapped him with the singing stone, but saved him from the Maranies, but helped kill his dragon self, but saved him again from the Maranies, taking a sword in the gut. Kanvar? Willing to die for him? Willing to kill him? Was Kanvar, friend or enemy?

A high-pitched wail shattered his disturbed thoughts. A human child sat amid a pile of sticks and torn cloth. A young one, maybe two years old, her ragged blond hair smudged with mud, her face scraped and bruised.

"Mama," the girl cried, holding her pudgy hands out to the air. "Mama, mama."

Rajan's mouth watered. She had plenty of meat on her bones, and one so young would be tender. He looked around for the mother, but no one straggled up from the rubble to claim the child.

He staggered over to her and picked her up. Her tattered yellow dress seeped water between his fingers. She came pre-seasoned with salt. Round brown eyes stared at him, and she stopped crying.

He bared his teeth and leaned toward her neck.

"Mama," she said, and pressed her body against his chest, snuggling her head into him, and wrapping little hands around his neck. Her skin was chilled, but the muscles beneath warm. A bundle of warmth in his arms, holding onto him.

He sucked in a sob and rubbed the gritty mud from her hair. How could he eat something so warm and fragile?

His stomach rumbled. He shook his head.

"Mama," the girl whispered. Her pudgy hands shifted to get a tighter hold on him.

"I'm not your mother," he rasped. "I am a red dragon, and I plan to eat you."

"Da?" She said. "Da, da?" She reached up to pat the stubble of hair that had grown on his chin since he'd shaved last. When? At the house he'd secured in Maran before the invasion of Varna. He'd pretended to be human then, to trick the humans, to take control. He'd eaten human food, stayed in a human house, slept in a human bed.

"Am I human?" he asked the little girl.

"Da," she said and snuggled closer to him.

He shuddered. Tears dripped down his cheek. "I'm a man, not a dragon. I'm a man." He hugged the child. His dragon self was gone. Dead. "I'm a man. I'm alone."

His breath caught. *Silverwave*, he called out with his mind. *Silverwave*? The silver serpent who had taken his bond could not be dead, or he would be dead with her, but he could not feel her. He had cut the rope and tricked her into leaving him, swimming to safety. Surely she must be safe somewhere out in the ocean.

"Please, mister. Help me please." A hand caught hold of the hem of his trousers. He looked down and saw an arm sticking out of a mound of mud and wood. A muffled female voice came from beneath it.

"Mama?" the little girl squeaked.

Rajan dropped to his knees and set the girl aside then took the woman's hand. "Hold on, just a moment. I'll get you out." His own voice sounded strange to him, ragged and warm. A human voice. He clawed the fallen boards away from the woman's face. A bruise had already started to swell and blacken one side.

"My baby? My little girl?"

"I have her right here." Rajan wished he could hold the child who had started crying again and dig the mother out at the same time. He forced his hands to move faster, throwing aside splintered wood, pawing away the mud until the woman was free enough she could crawl out of the rubble and over to her child. She enveloped the little girl in her arms and lay there shaking.

Around them, others were stirring. Those who could stand drew themselves up and surveyed the damage. So many fallen houses. So many trapped and hurting people. Their thoughts tore at Rajan's mind. He threw up a shield to protect himself from them as he had done in the dragon's lair. The human prisoners had cried so piteously, but his dragon self would not let him help them. But his red dragon self was gone, dead, killed by Kumar. He was free now to do as he wished. He shivered as a cold ocean breeze blew across his mind. Nothing and no one controlled it now. Except himself.

"Everyone," Rajan called. "All of you who can walk, come over here. We need to start pulling people out."

The people stared at him, dazed, unmoving.

"Come here, now," he commanded, putting enough power into his voice that the listeners responded without realizing his suggestion was controlling them.

Four men and two women, all of them bruised and scraped but well enough to move around, gathered at his command.

"We'll start here and work out in a spiral. You two, get those sticks there as levers. ladies, gather those boards as braces. You'll put them down beneath the rubble as these men pry it up, to hold up the load while we remove the people who are trapped. You two," he pointed to the final men, "pull people out from beneath the rubble. Gently, their neck or backs might be damaged." He relied on memories of his training at the dragon hunter complex in Daro to guide his plan on how to rescue the people trapped beneath the rubble.

"What will you do?" One of the men asked. He was a strong man, with broad shoulders and shaggy black hair and beard. His name tumbled from his mind into Rajan's.

"Good question, Frederick."

The man gasped and stepped back. "You're a Naga?" A look of fear crossed his face. He dropped to one knee. "Forgive me, Master. Whatever you command, we will do."

Rajan grinned, enjoying being in control. Everyone should bow to him like that. Then he grimaced. That was how his red dragon self had thought. He wasn't sure if that's how he wanted to think anymore. He glanced up at the white palace beside the river. One of the walls had crumbled and several of the towers fallen into heaps. A single golden flag still flapped in the wind. There were Nagas here, it seemed. And Kumar had been right about them being like the ones at Stonefountain.

"Get up, Frederick," Rajan said. "We don't have time for that sort of thing. We have people to save. The problem is finding where they are buried. Fortunately, I *am* a Naga. If they're conscious, I can sense them. We can find them, and we can get them out."

"Thank you, Master Naga, for your help. We are indebted to you." Another man by the name of Henry said. The others chimed in, agreeing.

Rajan glanced at the palace again, sweeping the skies for the ripple of Great Gold dragons taking flight. Where were the other Nagas? Why weren't they out here helping as well? No matter. He had more important things to take care of, human lives to save.

The work went slowly, fallen house by fallen house. Person by person. The living he grouped together, binding their wounds with what bandages he could make of scattered clothing, comforting them with what blankets he could find. The dead they laid out in a row of bodies elsewhere. He thought it would be a good idea to cover them, but he needed whatever cloth they could find for the living. The sound of crying never ceased. Too many people dead. Too many people hurt. A whole city to save.

He worked through the day and into the night, cursing that he could not see in the darkness. His red dragon self could see in the dark. But he was human now, and he could not. Not with his eyes anyway. He could still feel the thoughts of those who were trapped and find his way to them. His tongue swelled with thirst and clung to the roof of his mouth. All he could taste was salt and fear and pain. So many people pinned in the darkness, running out of air, hungry and thirsty and frightened. He had to get to them. His muscles burned as he heaved aside a heavy beam and started on a pile of rocks. His teams of priers and bracers had stopped when the sun set. But he could not stop. Too many people would die before morning if he did not reach them. Already, thoughts were fading out, people passing from this life because he could not get to them in time.

He got a man out from under the broken hut. There were two children with him. Dead, both of them, but the man lived. Rajan helped the man over to the other living and carried the children one by one to lay out beside the dead. The man stared at him through the darkness, too hurt and stunned to register that his children were dead. He thought only of his wife. Where was she? She'd gone dockside to buy fresh fish for dinner. Rajan's head spun, living his memories of her, searching the darkness for her mind, finding nothing. There was nothing left of the docks. The wave had hit them with its greatest force.

Rajan stumbled and fell to his knees, too weak, tired, and hungry to get back up.

Soft fingers curled around his arm. "Master Naga, you need to rest." It was the woman he had rescued first. Her voice was soothing. She carried the child on her hip and leaned over him. "Come sit with us. There is some water. We uncovered a well that was not too polluted by the great wave."

"How can I rest? People are dying." Rajan's voice sounded far away, his mind lost in the chaos of other people's thoughts.

"How can you save them if you don't?"

Rajan pulled his arm away from her and tried to get up, but his shaking legs would not hold him, and he fell forward, scraping his arm and chest on a pile of broken bricks.

The woman left him and came back with Henry and Frederick. They got him to his feet and helped him back to the survivor camp. They'd lit a fire. He couldn't imagine how with all the wood so wet, but they let him down by it, and the woman pressed a wooden cup of water into his hands.

Rajan took a sip and swallowed. Bit by bit, he rebuilt the shields around his mind, cutting it off from people in the city.

The woman sat down beside him. Her long hair was tangled. The firelight played off her bruised face. Her husband had been among the dead. She had cried most of the day while she helped bind broken bones and bandage the wounded. The tears had left streaks down the mud on her face. She shivered. Rajan scooted closer to her and put an arm around her shoulders to warm her.

She stiffened.

He jerked his arm back and edged away. "I-I'm sorry. I have no right. You looked cold."

The woman pressed her sleeping daughter to her chest and stared at him. What was she thinking? He did not know, he'd built his shields too thick and didn't dare take them down. He could not stand to die over and over again as those still trapped in the rubble succumbed to their wounds or the lack of air.

"You are different," she said.

"Different? Of course I'm different; I'm a Naga. I'm sorry I am, but I can't change it. I tried to kill myself, but my brother wouldn't let me. I guess he can't stop me now. I can't feel him anywhere. If he were alive, if he were awake, I could find him. *Him* I would feel above anyone else except my dragon." Rajan shuddered. "I can't feel her either. I am alone."

The woman blinked and touched his arm. "Different than other Nagas."

Rajan took her hand in his. He'd been married once, held a woman before. But no, that was not him. That was the farmer he'd stolen the memories from on the coast of Maran, Edward of Longshire, Edward who he'd made into a Maran senator, and then Prime Minister. He'd had a wife,

Cynthia. He'd left her behind in Longshire when he'd gone to the capital.

This woman's hands were delicate. So easy to crush and devour as a dragon. Perhaps even as a human he could hurt her. Her mind, of course, he could bend to any whim. He could make her want to let him put his arm around her.

A moan escaped his lips. He dropped her hand and turned away. "Leave me alone," he whispered, careful to be sure it had no impact upon her mind. "I don't want to hurt you."

"I don't believe you would hurt me."

Rajan took another swallow of water. There was a little salt in it, but not too much to keep it from quenching his thirst. "Sometimes I cannot control my powers. I have hurt people in the past, and I can't change that. I have been . . . evil." What else could he call a monster who devoured human flesh?

The woman shifted closer to the fire and stroked her daughter's hair. "Today you were not evil."

"One day in a long evil life. If you knew the things I've done, you would run and not look back, and wish you could wipe all knowledge of me from your mind." Rajan set down the empty cup and spread his palms to the fire. Part of him wanted to climb into the center of it and bask in the glowing coals.

Silence fell between them for a moment. The fire snapped and crackled. Around the fire, the other weary survivors of earthquake and flood slept.

"What is your name?" the woman asked.

I am fire. I am dragon, he thought. "Rajan," he said aloud.

"Rajan," the woman said with a smile on her lips. "My name is Dove, and this is Eleanor." She hugged her little girl to her as she slid over to him and laid her head on his chest. "And I *am* cold."

He put his arm back around her shoulders. "I'm sorry about your husband."

She let out a sob.

"Sh," he said, gently rubbing her forehead. "Sleep. Be at peace." He let his power like a gentle curtain slip her into dreamless slumber. Afterward he stared for a long time at the burning flames, wishing he were back home in the heart of the volcano.

## Chapter Nine

**Rajan woke before dawn** the next morning. The city was hushed by fog that rolled in off the ocean. He shivered and rubbed the dew off his bare chest and arms. The fire had gone out. Dove and Eleanor slept beside him. They'd kept each other warm the best they could in the night. Now he rose and moved away.

People watched him, their faces gray in the fog. He opened his mind enough to hear their thoughts. They feared him and wondered at him. Where had he gotten such gruesome scars? Why was he there, a Naga consorting with the lowest of people? Touching them. Helping them. Spending the night with them when surely there was food and heat and fresh water in the palace. Soft beds with fluffy blankets and every other comfort imaginable.

He sent his thoughts out for Silverwave and felt her stirring, sluggish, disoriented. She lay in a cave at the base of a reef out beyond the bay. He tried to speak to her, but she was too confused to understand his words. Her body hurt where she'd been dashed against the reef. He wished he could do something for her, but what? He could not go where she was.

He turned his attention back to the humans. "The sun will be up soon," he said. "We have work to do." So many people left to save, those that had survived the night.

Frederick got to his feet and squared his shoulders. "Where do we start, Master? What is it you seek here?"

Rajan looked from Frederick to the rest of the survivors in the camp. Some two hundred of them had gathered under his protection. "I seek the welfare of the people of this city, and . . . my brother. He was with me in a boat out on the water when the great wave came. We are twins. He looks like me, except he doesn't. He is not a Naga and has aged into an old man while I stayed young. But you will know him. Our eyes are the same. Our faces, though he doesn't have this scar." Rajan rubbed his cheek. "He wears red dragonscale armor and carries a heavy crossbow. He must be unconscious, or dead, for I cannot sense his mind. But if you see him, please, call me immediately."

"Yes, Master." Frederick motioned to the other men, those well enough to continue to look for survivors. They split into teams and went back to work, searching through the rubble of the outer city. Rajan went with them, guiding their efforts. There were fewer living left to be pulled to safety. The fog lifted slowly, allowing the pale sun to shine through. The scent of refuse and salt and mud hung heavily on the air.

Rajan's work crews stopped and turned back when they reached a street that separated the flattened hovels from larger stone houses. The walls of many of the more sturdy homes were still intact, though the wooden roofs had collapsed inward. Families sat dazed in the street, staring at their broken homes. Others toiled through the rubble searching for family members caught when the roofs collapsed. Rajan could feel them there, pinned beneath stone and wood, more living than remained in the wreck of the poorer part of the city.

"Why have you turned back?" Rajan asked his men. "There are people across the street who need our help."

Henry spit on the ground and pointed to a pile of dead bodies at the corner.

Rajan strode over to them and realized that they were all rough-looking men from the outer city. Their bodies did not have the crushed bones and bruises of those who had died in the quake, or the blue lips and bloated skin of those who had drowned. Livid stab wounds and sword slashes marred their bodies. A sign propped up against the corpses read, *Looters Will Die.*

Rajan recoiled.

A pair of men in black clothes with gold trim up the sides of the legs and across the shoulders marched down the street beyond. When they saw Rajan, they drew their swords and advanced on him. Behind him, Rajan felt his work crews melt away back to the outer city where they wouldn't be seen.

Rajan checked to make sure his own sword was loose enough in its sheath he could draw it easily, then he folded his arms across his chest and waited for the men. From their minds he found out they were part of the city watch, which had been given charge of search and rescue and security for the wealthier parts of the city.

"You there, move along," one of the men ordered.

Rajan remained in place. "The people of the outer city need food and water, shelter, bandages, healers. You call them looters, but they are only desperate to stay alive. We need your help."

"Get going, or you'll join that pile there," the second man said.

Rajan shook his head. "The two of you together couldn't beat me." Even if he didn't use his powers on them. He had practiced all his life with the sword, learning from dragon hunters in Daro and then staying in shape with the weapon during the long years in the dragon's lair. What else did he have to do there but kill and eat, after all?

"You don't stand a chance," the man said.

Rajan grinned and drew his sword. "I'll tell you what. Let's fight. If you win, you kill me. If I win, you hand over some of the emergency supplies you've been delivering to the richies."

The two men stopped on the far side of the street. The first pressed a whistle to his lips and blew a shrill note. The sound of running feet slapped the flagstones and a dozen more of the city watch raced out from adjoining streets. Most had swords. Several raised loaded crossbows.

Rajan rolled his eyes and sheathed his sword.

The first two men smirked at him, full of pride and their own perceived power.

"Put your weapons down," Rajan snapped.

The whole flock of city watchmen dropped their weapons at their feet. Their eyes widened in shock.

"Now get your proud black butts moving and start distributing food and supplies to the residents of the outer city." Rajan made sure that every man present would be forced to obey his command. Then he went back to re-gather his own crews and put them back to work.

At noon, Dove found him pulling children from what remained of a humble schoolhouse. More children than he would have guessed had survived, mostly because the walls had been paper thin and the roof no more than oiled canvas stretched across the frame. The children were frightened and confused, and it took all his concentration to calm them, identify their parents and homes from their thoughts, and match them up with living relatives.

"Rajan, here." Dove pressed a bread crust into his hands as soon as the girl he carried sank into the arms of her uncle, the only other person in her family to survive. "The city watch has come. Finally they're starting to help us. No one thought they would, but Frederick said you made them."

Rajan chuckled and bit off a chunk of bread.

Dove frowned. "There could be trouble. Did His Lordship put you in charge of the watch?"

"His Lordship?" Rajan glanced up to the palace. A ripple of gold launched from one of the arched windows and streaked across the sky. The Nagas were moving, finally.

"Lord Theodoric, the great and beneficent ruler of Navgarod under His Majesty of Stonefountain. Of course His Lordship. His Naga Guards command the city watch. So, unless you're one of them, and I can't imagine you are from the way you dress and talk, His Lordship might object to your interfering with his men."

Rajan rolled his shoulders and took another bite of bread. All his childhood he'd been trained to hate Nagas to despise the brutality and slavery of Stonefountain. Then he'd bonded with the Great Red dragon and come to instead hate all the dragon hunters who brutally murdered the Nagas. He'd come so close to destroying them all, to making all the humans pay for what they'd done at Stonefountain and to the Naga children born after.

Now by strange chance he'd come to a place where the Nagas still ruled. The dragon hunter part of him wanted to fight them, to kill them all and free these people who they claimed lordship over. Another part of him wanted to congratulate Lord Theodoric on staying in power despite the fall of Stonefountain, on running an efficient and organized city. Of course the aid would go to the wealthy first. Well, the Nagas first, then the wealthy and powerful. Of what use would saving the rabble of the outer city be? They were nothing more than empty mouths to feed, lazy, weak. So much like the humans the red dragon kept in his cages. Only once had Rajan tried to help them. Once when the red dragon had first taken him from Kundiland and flown him to the lair on the island.

Rajan ran his hand across the mottled burn scars that covered most of his torso. He'd paid a painful price for that and never tried to help the humans again. Never, all those years. He'd watched so much pain and suffering, caused so much of it.

Rajan swallowed the last of the bread and drew his sword. "I don't have a problem with His Lordship. If His Lordship has a problem with me helping people, then he will have a problem indeed. I am the most powerful Naga alive. I conquered Maran and Varna by myself. I was ruler of the Western World. The throne of Stonefountain was in my grasp. If he fights me, he will regret it."

Dove put her hands on her hips and cocked her head to the side. "You, the king at Stonefountain?"

"I was this close before my brother and grandnephew stopped me." Rajan held up his thumb and finger so only a sliver of light passed between them. "Turns out my grand-nephew is second heir to the throne himself and objected to my claiming it." Rajan laughed and put the sword away.

"Ah but I hate that boy as much as I like him. My brother's daughter married the king. Who would have imagined that ever happening? Not I."

"You're from the land beyond the Western Sea? You're from Stonefountain?" Dove stared at him wide-eyed, all sassiness forgotten.

"Where's your daughter?" Rajan asked, changing the subject.

"Safe, back at the camp with my sister. We found my sister this morning, still alive."

"Good. Mind if I have some of that water?" Rajan gestured to the gourd of water she had slung over her shoulder.

"Oh, yes. Sorry." She handed it to him and he drank. It still tasted brackish, but he didn't care.

"Frederick asked me to find you and bring you to him," Dove said. "He found someone he thinks might be your brother, but he's not sure."

"Where? Show me." Thoughts of Lord Theodoric and Stonefountain scattered from his mind as he followed Dove through the rubble. She led him though the mess until they came close to the outer city wall. It had been built of white limestone like most of the nicer buildings in the city, but large sections of it had crumbled. They found Henry and Frederick and their team of rescuers up next to a fallen section. A splash of red color set Rajan into a sprint. There was a form there, laying amidst the broken stones, the red dragonscale armor recognizable even at a distance. Rajan raced toward his brother's side, but Frederick caught him and held him back.

"Wait. We didn't dare move him. His back is twisted. It may be broken. Be careful."

Frederick was right. Kumar lay twisted half on his back, half on his side like the wave had slammed his back, where his heavy crossbow was strapped, against the wall hard enough to tear down the stones, hard enough to snap Kumar's vertebrae in half. His face was bruised. His eyes closed. Rajan could not see his chest rise or fall with breath.

"No. Kumar." Rajan pulled away from Frederick and went carefully to his brother's side. "Kumar, please." He pressed his fingers against Kumar's neck, looking for a pulse, but could not feel it. He shifted his fingers, pressed a little harder. "Kumar?" There it was, the faintest flutter of life.

"He's alive." Barely, but for how long Rajan couldn't guess. Carefully, he straightened his body out on his side, unbuckled the crossbow harness and moved the weapon and its bolts out of the way. Then he unfastened Kumar's armor and eased it open to reveal Kumar's back. A massive bruise spread down his spine from just below his shoulder blades to the small of his back. The center was red and inflamed.

"It would be better if he were dead," Frederick said, "or died quickly now. He'll never walk again."

"Silence!" Rajan yelled.

The entire work crew and every person and animal for half a mile fell quiet. So quiet Rajan could here his brother draw in a ragged breath. Rajan had used his powers too much. He might have hurt people, but he was hardly aware of that as he pawed through Kumar's belt pouches and pockets. It had to be there somewhere. Kumar had used it to heal Rajan's neck.

His fingers closed around the vial of dragon saliva. His brother could not die. Would not die. Rajan would not let him. He opened the vial and poured all of the contents out into his cupped hand then rubbed it along Kumar's spine, gently covering the bruised and swollen skin, massaging the saving liquid into the muscles, letting it seep down to the bones. Pressing with both hands in a gentle but firm motion to realign Kumar's spine.

Kumar regained consciousness and cried out in pain.

"Here," Rajan ordered Frederick. "Help me move him off the rocks and lay him flat."

Though they were careful to keep his head and back in line and lay him flat on his stomach, Kumar cried out again as they moved him.

"It's all right," Rajan reassured him. "You're going to be all right."

Kumar's thoughts flooded into Rajan's mind, disoriented and confused. The pain from his back threatened to drag him into unconsciousness once more.

"Where am I," Kumar said through gritted teeth.

"The city. The great wave drove us ashore. You've been hurt. Lie still."

"My hands are tingling. I can't feel my legs."

Rajan grimaced and glanced over at Frederick who had not spoken since Rajan had commanded his silence. In fact, no one had. The entire work crew stood still, staring at him.

Rajan swore. "All right. You can talk now. Do whatever you want." He released their minds from his compulsion and turned back to his brother. "Kumar. I rubbed the dragon saliva on your back. Will it work? On broken bones, I mean. I can't remember what they taught us." Rajan had paid more attention to lessons on how to hunt and kill than how to heal.

Kumar groaned, lifted his right hand, stretched his fingers, then balled them into a fist. "My back is broken?"

"Maybe. Maybe it's just bruised." Rajan tried to convince himself that was the case.

"Yes. It's broken," Frederick said.

Rajan felt like forcing Frederick to silence again, but stopped himself. He couldn't hide the truth from his brother. Kumar was too smart for that.

"Did you use all the dragon saliva I had?" Kumar asked.

"Yes. All of it. There wasn't much left." Rajan thought of all the injured people back at the survivor camp. If he had more saliva, he could help so many people.

"It won't be enough," Kumar said. Kumar tested the movement of his other hand and then lay still. "Where is Silverwave? How close are we to the ocean?"

"She's hurt. Out by a reef. I can't get her to talk to me."

"We'll need her saliva." Kumar winced and closed his eyes. "A lot of it."

"Then I'll get more," Rajan said. "Somehow."

## Chapter Ten

**Rajan glanced across the** flattened city to the ocean. *Silverwave*, he called.

Silverwave moaned and fanned her wing fins.

*Can you swim to shore where the docks were? I need your help.*

*Rajan*? Her thoughts were faint and troubled.

*Yes, it's Rajan, of course. Who else would be talking to you? Are you all right?* Rajan buckled Kumar's crossbow onto his own back, amazed that it was still intact. But the polished wood was harder than human bones. Even the bolts were still in the individual leather slots that held them in place along the straps of the harness. He felt strange wearing his brother's weapons, the crossbow now as well as the sword, but he couldn't leave the crossbow lying around where anyone could take it. Kumar would likely never forgive him if it got stolen.

*I am . . . recovering,* Silverwave said. *But if I swim to shore the humans may try to kill me. I do not relish being struck by another harpoon in my lifetime.*

*I'll meet you there and make sure no one is able to harm you.* Rajan looked around for a piece of wood big enough to carry Kumar on without jarring his back. He saw a fallen door in some rubble and called Frederick and Henry to help him get it and slide Kumar onto it.

"Carry him to the camp. Carefully," Rajan said. "Please. If I have been any service to the rest of you at all, do this for me. Keep him safe until I get back. I'm going after some more Great dragon saliva for him and for the other wounded. Dove, I'll need that gourd you've been using to carry water."

Dove pressed the gourd into his hand and whispered. "I don't care what Frederick says. I'm sure your brother will recover."

"Of course he'll recover," Rajan said, trying to convince himself. He knelt beside Kumar and pressed a hand against his forehead. Kumar was still conscious but in a lot of pain. "I'm going to get some more dragon saliva. Just hold on, all right?"

Kumar's answer was drowned out by a chorus of shrill screeches from the air.

Kumar jerked in surprise. "Raptors," he hissed. "Rajan, look to the sky. What kind are they?"

Rajan jumped to his feet and glanced across the outer city. Flying black lesser dragons with crimson on the undersides of their wings swarmed out of the forest and flew toward the outer city.

"Redwinged raptors. Dozens of them." Rajan's heart dropped to his toes as the feral dragons filled the air with their shrill cries.

"Makes sense," Kumar said. His voice was hoarse and he had barely enough strength to speak. "They are scavengers. This whole place stinks of death. Of course they'll come."

Henry swore. "The dead. We haven't had time to bury them. But these redwings aren't scavengers. They come to the scent of blood and once they've smelled it they go into a bloodlust and kill anything, everything. The Naga Guard usually keeps them miles away from the city."

Rajan scanned the sky, looking for ripples of gold of the Great Gold dragons in flight. He'd seen one earlier, but nothing now.

"We have to get back to camp and protect the women and children," Frederick said.

"My daughter." Dove ran back toward the camp followed by the other workers.

Henry hesitated. "Master Naga, you have the only weapon that will be of any use against the raptors. Come help us."

Rajan reached for the crossbow but stopped and glanced down at Kumar. "I can't leave him. This close to the edge of the city they'll take him first."

"If we try to carry him with us, they'll kill all three of us." Henry grabbed up a pair of stones. "I guess we make a stand here, you and I. They'll kill us, of course, but maybe it will buy time for the others."

"You're a brave man." Rajan pulled the crossbow from the harness and grabbed a bolt to load into it. Then realized the weapon had two strings, two tracks. "A double crossbow? It's beautiful. I've never seen anything like it."

"Shut up and shoot the dumb dragons," Kumar snarled. "Or give it to me so I can."

"No. You stay down. Don't move." Rajan loaded the crossbow and climbed the rubble up to the top of a section of the wall that had not collapsed. The swarm of redwings flapped toward him in a wheeling maelstrom, their cries deafening him. As they grew close to the city, they split apart, and Rajan realized most would fly past him on either side. Two crossbow bolts could not stop dozens of winged dragons in a city full of blood.

*Stay back!* he shouted into their minds.

Unlike human minds, the lesser dragon minds were not filled with ordered thoughts, human words and Great dragon speech meant nothing to them. They were creatures of instinct and all their instinct cried that an open feast lay before them.

Screeching, the bulk of the dragons sped past Rajan. Only the closest five recognized the target he had presented himself as on the wall. They dove toward him, clawing at each other over who would claim their prize.

Rajan waited until they were close enough he could be sure to hit them. He'd never been as good with the crossbow as Kumar. At last he let off two bolts, one after the other, striking the closest redwing in the eye and another in the chest. The other three startled up at the sound of the crossbow firing, and seeing two other men on the ground below dove at the new targets of their frenzied hunger.

Henry pelted them with his stones while Rajan reloaded. The rocks bounced off their scaly black hides, angering the dragons.

One ripped at Henry with his talons, slicing his arm. Another landed beside Kumar, saliva spraying from its jaws as it roared and snapped at Kumar's flesh. But its teeth never made contact. Kumar lifted his arm and smashed it in the face with a broken board.

Rajan fired again, and the redwing slumped down beside Kumar. The remaining two dragons had Henry in the air by then, locked in their talons, fighting over who would devour him. Rajan let go another bolt and one of the dragons dropped. But the remaining one, shrieking in triumph, flew away with Henry.

*Put him down*, Rajan ordered the redwing, but its blood-lusted mind barely registered the command.

Gasping, Rajan reloaded the crossbow. There had to be some way he could control the swarm of lesser dragons, but their thoughts were all twisted around blood and hunger. He shuddered. Blood and hunger were sensations he knew well. He'd experienced the need, the drive, the lust. The volcanic red dragon had not been so different than these.

*You are hungry*, he cried out with his mind to the dozens of redwings that were attacking and feasting on the city's residents. *You are hungry for blood and meat.* He basked in their bloodlust, letting it swell and grow, take over and control their minds with him at the center of it. *You are hungry and there is the sweetest kill, the juiciest blood, here with me. To me, to me. I will fill all of your needs, I will satiate your hunger. Nothing will fill you like my flesh. You hunger for nothing but one man. Come to me!*

The redwings twisted up from the rubble and wheeled in the sky, crazed with hunger. Their focus turned as one toward Rajan, and they swooped toward him.

"Shoot. It worked," Rajan muttered. He was glad he'd managed to pull the redwings away from the people in the city, but now they would come kill him. He could not possibly fight so many by himself. He let loose the last two crossbow shots he had time for, then dropped the crossbow and drew his sword.

“Come on then, monsters!” he yelled. “Taste my blood. Feel my sword.”

The redwings converged in the air above him, dozens of ravenous lesser dragons intent on the same prize, a single man on a wall with a sword. He could not hope to kill more than a couple of them before they shredded him. In desperation he twisted their minds one final turn. They couldn't all have him. They must kill their competitors for his blood.

In a tornado of wings and claws and teeth, the redwing raptors tore into each other. Blood rained from the sky as the dragons brawled. Fighting and killing one another over the prize below. Rajan retreated from the wall to get better footing on the ground so he could fend off those dragons that fought their way past the others and dove at him. Their talons raked his back and arms and his muscles burned at the effort of defending his life. But one by one the dragons fell dead, killed by their own kind or sliced through by him.

Two of the redwings broke free of the crowd together and came at him. One straight for his face, the other at his back. He sliced off the head of the one in front of him, but the one behind got his talons locked on Rajan's flesh and lifted him into the air with a roar of victory.

Rajan screamed.

The air in front of him rippled gold, and a blast of sparkling golden breath hit the raptor in the face. It let out a mewling squeal and fluttered to the ground, releasing Rajan.

A crossbow twanged, and a bolt took the dragon in the chest. Rajan looked up and saw the air was full of ripples and Great Gold dragon joy breath. The remaining redwings broke off the fight and floated off out of the city or landed. Crossbows fired, killing those that landed.

Air gusted in Rajan's face as a Great Gold dragon settled onto a rubble pile several yards away. A Naga slid off its back, handed a crossbow to the dragon, and walked toward Rajan. He wore a golden vest over a white silk shirt. His golden hair was tied back with a diamond-studded leather thong. His eyes were hard with wisdom brought on by age, though his skin had not been touched by time. He wore a sword at his side.

"So you're the renegade Naga," he said. Pride and power washed from his mind. "How dare you set foot in this city? You challenge my authority, twisting the minds of my own men to your whims?"

Rajan sheathed his sword and picked up the fallen crossbow. A glance to the side assured him that Kumar still lay where he had before, and the raptors had not succeeded in harming him. "I had no desire to come here, believe me. I was caught by the wave and dashed ashore or I would not have come within miles of this place. But I'm glad I did, because while you've sat tucked away comfortable and secure in your palace, I have been working to save your people."

"How dare you?" The golden Naga drew his sword. "I am Captain Vitra. I have commanded the Naga Guard under Lord Theodoric for hundreds of years. No man in this city other than My Lord is more powerful than I."

Rajan laughed and loaded Kumar's crossbow. "I dare, because I speak the truth. I am not afraid of you. I am Rajan, bound to a Great Red volcanic dragon. No one in the world is more powerful than I am."

In the back of his mind, Silverwave winced. She wasn't a tenth as powerful as the red dragon had been. He no longer wielded the power that he once had.

Captain Vitra lashed out at Rajan with his mind, attempting to tear through his shields and bring him to his knees with a strike of pain that would have shivered any other man.

Rajan was no stranger to pain. Pain he could handle. He rebuffed Vitra's mind, then stabbed with his own power at Vitra's. Their two wills locked, neither able to overcome the other.

Rajan laughed and pulled his power back, breaking away from Vitra's mind.

Captain Vitra reset his grip on his sword and glared at Rajan. "I have a dozen men in the air. Do you think you are more powerful than all of us combined?"

"Not likely. Let's call it even. Together we've defeated the redwings. How about you go your way, and I go mine? Give me an hour and I'll be gone from this city forever."

"No. You have broken our law. The punishment is execution. I cannot let you go."

"What law have I broken?"

"Only the most basic law of our existence. No Naga will bond with any dragon other than a Great Gold, and then only with the blessing of His Lordship. You are a renegade. You think you can live outside our laws and beyond Lord Theodoric's rule?"

A long-building fire of anger and resentment burst from Rajan. "Where were your gold dragons when I came down with the fever? Where was Lord Theodoric when my own father and uncle shot me down like a diseased bovinder? Why weren't you there to stop the red dragon when he took me, forced his blood down my throat and tore away my existence? Where were you through the decades of torture and fire?" Rajan let out a bark of derisive laugher. "You call me a renegade? I call you a coward. Where were you and all your men, where was Lord Theodoric when Stonefountain fell and they slaughtered the rest of us? Hiding here on the safe side of the world, letting generations of helpless Naga children perish in the human's endless purge of our kind? I condemn you, all of you, and your Lord. You're the ones who should be executed. Cowards. Honorless. Fatherless wyrmlings."

Cursing, Vitra charged, intending to cut Rajan down with the sword.

Rajan raised the crossbow and pointed it at Vitra's heart. "Another step and you die."

Vitra froze. "There are a dozen crossbows aimed at you this moment. You release that bolt, and you will not take another breath."

"Then we will die together. I'm all right with that."

"Rajan." Kumar groaned and lifted a hand toward him. "Don't do anything stupid."

A shock went through Rajan. He'd forgotten his injured brother for a moment in the heat of his anger.

"What does it matter? They plan to kill me anyway." Bitterness laced Rajan's voice.

Vitra's dragon sucked in a breath.

"Don't do it!" Rajan shouted at the dragon. "I promise you my finger will pull this trigger before your joy breath envelops me."

The dragon let out a guttural growl.

Rajan licked his lips and glanced once more at Kumar. No matter what, the Nagas would kill Rajan. There was no way out of this for him, but maybe he could turn it to Kumar's advantage.

"We are at an impasse," Rajan said, his throat tight. "Let me suggest a resolution." He pointed to Kumar. "Have your dragon heal my brother's back and I will lay down my weapons and submit to execution."

Vitra looked down and noticed Kumar for the first time. "That man is your brother?" Was it consternation or derision in Vitra's voice?

"He's not a Naga and has aged like a normal human, but he is my twin."

"And if my dragon heals his back, you put yourself into my custody without a fight?"

"Yes. Just heal him."

"Swear by Stonefountain."

"I swear by the waters of Stonefountain and all its power I will submit to execution."

"Very well, Telanies." Vitra motioned to his dragon.

Sunlight flashed as Telanies slid over to Kumar and bathed his back with saliva, licking the wound until the livid bruises faded and the enflamed muscles settled.

Rajan swallowed, pivoted away from Vitra, and dropped to his knees by his brother. "Kumar," he said, laying the crossbow beside him and shrugging out of the harness.

Kumar moved his hand just enough to catch hold of Rajan's arm. "Little brother, don't leave me."

"I've no choice." He unbuckled the sword belt and pressed the weapon into Kumar's hand. "Live for me. Hunt dragons for me. Be as great as I always wanted to be."

"Rajan, I can't lose you again."

A sword pressed against Rajan's back. He was grabbed roughly, his hands twisted behind him and bound there. Vitra threw him down in the rubble. "You will pay for every word you have spoken. No one questions my honor without suffering for it."

Great Gold dragon claws closed around Rajan and swept him into the air.

Below him, Kumar moaned and sat up. "Rajan!" he yelled, reaching to the sky.

## Chapter Eleven

**Bensharie landed on the** sandy beach and flopped down on his belly, lowering his head to the ground and closing his eyes. Kanvar slid off his back, reveling in Kundiland's moist air and heat. Above the beach, the jungle spread out in front of him, leaves and vines and towering trees whose canopies reached to the sky. Scaly macaws filled the air with the flutter of colorful wings and their piercing cries. An undertone of black monkey chatter welcomed him home.

Kanvar patted Bensharie's shoulder. The exhausted muscles rippled beneath his touch. "We made it, Bensharie. We've come all the way home to the western coast of Kundiland.

*Too bad Dharanidhar is far away on the east coast*, Bensharie mumbled.

"Right." Kanvar sat down and leaned against Bensharie. "And he hasn't caught anything to eat at all today. But you can go no farther at the moment. Get some rest."

*Kanvar!* Devaj's urgent call in his head startled Kanvar to alertness. *Thank the fountain you're here. Stay right there. I'm coming.*

*Oh don't worry, we're not going anywhere.* Kanvar sucked in the scent of molten gold from Bensharie's scales and verdant plant life from the jungle. While he waited, he fiddled with his father's sword. Devaj had felt unusually upset. The feeling was strange coming from his calm and patient brother.

The air rippled above the trees, and Elkatran settled onto the beach beside Bensharie. Crooning, Devaj's dragon nuzzled his younger brother.

Kanvar struggled to his feet in time to be caught up in a hug from his brother as well.

"Kanvar. Kanvar." Moisture rimmed Devaj's eyes.

"Devaj, really. We're fine. There's nothing to cry over." Kanvar pulled away from his brother and straightened his armor and weapons.

Devaj cleared his throat, rubbed the moisture from his eyes, and stared off into the jungle for a moment while he got a hold of himself. "Kanvar," he said again, but his voice cracked.

A feeling of dread swept over Kanvar. Devaj's worry did not seem to be directed at him at all. "What is it? What's wrong?"

Devaj cleared his throat again. His hands gripped his golden robes. He would not look Kanvar in the eyes as he said, "It's Rajahansa. Father sent me away from the palace to take Eska and Denali to the village. I visited Raahi as well, to make sure he was all right. While I was gone, Rajahansa started gathering a dragon army to fight the humans. He thinks the humans will come because you disobeyed him and went after that Naga."

Kanvar bristled. "That Naga is our granduncle. Grandfather Raza's twin brother, Rajan. He was taken and bound against his will to a Great Red volcanic dragon. The dragon enslaved his mind and used his power. It had to be stopped."

"Yes. But now the humans know we exist. Rajahansa insists they are coming for us."

"Unfortunately they are." Kanvar hated to confirm his brother's fears, but Rajahansa and Amar needed to be told immediately. "The entire Maran army, and the Varnan army, and all the dragon hunters. They are coming here, and they know the location of the jungle village. We must evacuate the village and abandon the palace."

Devaj gasped and turned to face Kanvar. No longer able to hold the tears back, they streamed down his face. "Kanvar. Rajahansa won't run. He's gathering an army to fight them. Do you understand what I'm saying? He's using his power to force all the Great dragons and lesser dragons to fight them. Forcing . . . power . . . Great Blues . . . he's gone to their nesting ground."

Kanvar stiffened and his hand closed on his sword hilt. "Father would never let him."

"Father tried to stop him. They argued. Rajahansa sprayed him with joy breath and chained him in the palace. I tried to free him, but father ordered me to run, to escape and find you. I barely got away before Rajahansa could take control of my mind and Elkatran's. Rajahansa has grown more powerful somehow, and he's changed." Devaj gripped Kanvar's arm with shaking hands. "Rajahansa, Haidar, and Liander have gone to the Great Blue nesting grounds to enslave the blue dragons. You have to stop them somehow."

"Devaj." Kanvar wrapped his good arm over his brother's shoulders.

Exhaustion fell away from Kanvar and formed into a single clear thought. Akshara's singing stone rested in the iron cook pot in the bag Kanvar carried.

Devaj shuddered. "Please, Kanvar. Do something. Rajahansa has turned on his own Naga. He's trying to enslave everyone."

"Devaj." Kanvar gave him a little shake, his pampered golden brother who had spent most of his life in the comfort of the golden palace and never known hardship. "Devaj, listen to me. I will stop Rajahansa. I promise. But I need your help. Bensharie is too tired to fly any more today, and Dharanidhar is too weak and too far away. I need you and Elkatran to fly me up to the blue dragon nesting ground."

"But Rajahansa's crazy. He'll kill us, or worse."

Kanvar eased away from his brother. Fear consumed Devaj's mind. Whatever had transpired in the palace was beyond Devaj's ability to cope. His thoughts were a hopeless tangle, and at the center of them a throbbing terror—Khalid.

Kanvar reached into the cloth bag at his side, eased the lid off the pot, and pulled out Akshara's singing stone. The wail of the suffering spirit trapped inside sliced through Kanvar's mind.

Devaj cried out and pressed his hands against his head.

Kanvar held the stone up in front of Devaj's face. "Rajahansa will be powerless. Now fly me up there, quickly. Come, Elkatran, let's go. It doesn't sound like we have much time." Kanvar returned the stone to the pot and walked over to Elkatran, motioning for the Great Gold dragon to lean down so he could climb onto his neck.

Elkatran complied, but Devaj remained where he stood. "What about father?"

"One problem at a time. He may be chained, but it's not like Rajahansa is going to kill him."

Devaj shuddered.

"Are you coming?" Kanvar asked.

Devaj glanced over at Bensharie. "I think perhaps someone should stay here and look after Bensharie. He's young, and he's flown a long way."

Kanvar smiled. "I think you're right, Devaj. You should stay here and make sure he's safe.

Devaj nodded, relief flooding his countenance.

*What about you? Elkatran*, Kanvar asked. *Are you brave enough to fly me up there?*

Elkatran let out a rumbling purr. *I will go gladly, but Devaj's fear is not his fault. His mind has not been the same since his visit to Stonefountain.*

Kanvar's gut twisted. Khalid, The Great Naga King of Stonefountain, had seized Devaj's mind and tried to inhabit his body. Kanvar's hand slipped into the bag and rested beside the iron pot close to Akshara's stone. Rajahansa he could face, but if he ever had to face Khalid in full power, Kanvar worried he would be just as paralyzed by fear as his brother.

Elkatran flapped his wings, launched into the air, and headed for the high mountains. Kanvar wished it were Dharanidhar that was taking him to face Rajahansa and Parmver's sons.

**By the time the** Great Gold dragon dropped Rajan on the flagstones in the courtyard of the white palace, blood from his raptor wounds slicked his naked torso. He hurt and he didn't care. Why should he care if he lost too much blood now? His only regret was that Silverwave would die with him. She should never have taken his bond. Poor dragon. Poor sweet dragon.

Captain Vitra ordered Rajan to his feet.

Rajan rose and squared his shoulders.

"What's this?" A voice cut across the courtyard.

Rajan turned to stare at the man who had spoken. He wore a white silk shirt like Captain Vitra, but it was torn and smudged with dirt. No gold vest. His hands were scraped and filthy. White limestone dust clung to his hair, which once may have been secured back like Vitra's, but now hung in a tangled mess. Stubble grew across his chin as if he'd not bothered to shave for two days. He looked older than Captain Vitra, but his eyes were troubled. He'd been striding across the courtyard but pulled up short at Rajan's arrival.

"A renegade Naga, making trouble in the city," Vitra said, hate and disgust dripping from his voice.

The man's brow furrowed as he looked more closely at Rajan. "Looks like he had an encounter with the redwings. Did you take care of them, Captain?"

"Yes, My Lord. They're dead."

"My Lord?" Rajan asked in surprise. "You're Lord Theodoric?" If this was Lord Theodoric, the man was nothing like Rajan would have expected.

"Silence." Captain Vitra slammed Rajan to the ground. "He claims he's bound to a Great Red Volcanic dragon."

Theodoric walked over to where Rajan lay face down on the flagstones, his hands still bound behind his back. His Lordship circled Rajan slowly then used his foot to roll Rajan onto his back and have a look at his torso.

Rajan glared up into his frowning face.

"Burn scars like that make me believe he's probably telling the truth," Theodoric said his voice mild and thoughtful. He squatted down to speak to Rajan up close. "A volcanic dragon? Why?"

"There weren't any other options, not that the dragon gave me any choice. He saw power and he took it." The taste of blood clung to Rajan's tongue and he forced back fiery memories of his time with the dragon. He tightened the shields around his own mind to keep out the probing thoughts Lord Theodoric aimed at him.

"Where is your dragon? Is he a threat to this city?" Theodoric asked.

"The red dragon is dead, killed by my brother to free me. A Great Silver serpent now carries my bond."

"He's mad," Captain Vita said. "Deranged. Dangerous. You should have seen him consorting with the redwings. I think he called them."

"You lying coward. I was defending innocent people from their attack. Hundreds of citizens would have died before you arrived had I not done it." Rajan tried to jump to his feet, but Captain Vitra slammed him back down and put a sword to his chest.

"Silence, renegade. You will only speak when His Lordship orders you to."

Theodoric straightened and wiped limestone dust from his hands. "We don't have time for this, Vitra. Heal his wounds. Lock him up. I'll deal with him later."

"He should be executed. Slowly and painfully. Let me do it right now. Then I can get back to my duties." Captain Vitra pressed the tip of the sword into Rajan's skin, drawing forth a bead of blood to add to the rest that covered him.

"Slowly . . . and painfully?" Theodoric looked troubled.

"He has disparaged my honor, and yours. He must pay," Vitra said.

The sword pressed deeper in Rajan's flesh, but Lord Theodoric grabbed Vitra's hand, stopping him. "I have children—" Theodoric swallowed hard. "—Naga children dying, trapped under rubble. You think I care about your honor? Lick his wounds closed, Telanies," Theodoric snapped at the dragon. "Vitra, lock him up and come help me. Send your men to patrol the city for predators. More are bound to come. We can't let this disaster destroy the people's faith in us." Theodoric pushed Vitra away from Rajan then strode off toward a fallen section of the palace.

Captain Vitra kicked Rajan in the side then sheathed his sword. "You will pay. I promise." He called one of his men down from the sky. A second gold dragon landed in the courtyard, and the man, in the same Naga Guard uniform as Vitra, hurried over.

"Lock him up, Garron," Vitra ordered, then followed Theodoric out of the courtyard.

Garron looked down at Rajan and swore in disgust. "Why do I always have to clean up the filth? Get up."

He dragged Rajan to his feet and forced him toward some stairs that led down below an intact portion of the palace. Vitra's dragon swiped Rajan's wounds with his tongue as he passed, then snorted and spit the blood out on the ground.

## Chapter Twelve

**Kanvar guided Elkatran across** the jungles of Kundiland and into the mountains. Ever since the Maranies had first settled Kundiland, driving the Great Blue dragons from their ocean front nesting grounds, the Great Blue dragons had hidden in a secret valley in the high mountains. The location of the valley had been unknown to the Great Gold dragons until Kanvar, attempting to save Devaj's life, had shown his father how to get there. Kanvar regretted that now. Not saving his brother, but betraying the location of the nesting grounds to Rajahansa.

He'd never imagined the Great Gold dragon could change so suddenly into a threat. But he should have known, Dharanidhar had shown him what the Great Gold dragons of Stonefountain had been like, the cruel task masters they'd become. Kanvar swore he would never let that happen to his Great Blue dragon pride whether he and Dharanidhar were in exile or not.

In the back of his mind, he felt Dharanidhar lumber to his feet and roar. Dharanidhar had given his word to Akshara himself never to let the Great Blue dragons become enslaved once again. He lit Akshara's cave with angry blue fire. *Fly to me first*, Dharanidhar said. *I will go with you to confront Rajahansa. This is my call, my duty. Come to me so we can fly up there together.*

*There's no time, Dhar. You're too far away and too weak. Just wait for me there. I'll come to you as soon as I deal with Rajahansa.*

*I'm not too weak. Not for this. I will fight the Great Gold dragon king to my dying breath.*

Kanvar grinned. *I'm not interested in dying today.* Ignoring Dharanidhar's demands, Kanvar urged Elkatran to fly as fast as possible to the cliffs overlooking the blue dragon valley. The valley was a bowl, shaped by an azure lake so blue it seemed as if someone had taken a scoop of the sky and settled it onto the ground. Over time the lake had receded to a jewel of water surrounded by high mountain meadows and ringed by cliffs in which the Great Blue dragons had delved their lairs.

When Elkatran landed on the high cliff overlooking the valley, Kanvar saw that the Great Blue dragons had come out of their lairs and amassed in a group on the meadow. Rajahansa stood on his hind legs before them, wings raised, head held high. Parmver's sons, Haidar and

Liander, flanked him on either side atop their dragons. The three Great Gold dragons and two Nagas were using all their power to twist the minds of the Great Blue dragons to their will.

*We will fight the humans*, Rajahansa thundered. *They will fall by the thousands beneath our claws and our fire.*

Anilon, the leader of the Great Blue dragon pride since Dharanidhar's departure, struggled to resist Rajahansa's compulsion. *We blue dragons fought the humans for a long time while you cowered away in your palace, but we had little success. If the humans are coming, they will bring ballistae that can drop a Great dragon with a single bolt. They will wear armor to protect themselves from our fire. If we fly out to meet them, we will be slaughtered. If you feel threatened, Rajahansa, you should retreat. Take your pride and your Nagas and fly away.*

*Silence!* Rajahansa sent a mental blow that shivered Anilon to his knees and snapped his jaws shut. *We will fight. You will fight. You cannot resist my commands, and if any of you try, you will receive the same punishment as your leader.*

Anilon let out a howl of pain and fell to his stomach thrashing in agony caused by Rajahansa's powerful mind. Anger burned through Kanvar. *Fly me down there, Elkatran.*

Elkatran trumpeted in reply and launched himself from the cliff. He dove to the meadow and landed between Anilon and Rajahansa then rose up to face his father, wings spread, teeth bared. *Leave the blue dragons alone.*

Rajahansa growled. *You dare defy me? My own son? You would side with that crippled abomination on your back?*

Kanvar reached into the bag and got hold of the cookpot lid.

*Father, this is wrong,* Elkatran said. *Don't let your fear of the humans turn you into something you are not. Anilon is right. We should find a new place to hide from the humans. We have time to get away.*

*No.* Rajahansa roared. *The time for running and hiding is past. We have let the humans rule this world for too long. The time of the dragons is now. Victory will be ours.*

Kanvar shuddered. Rajahansa without Amar's calming influence was not a dragon to trifle with, and yet he must.

"You abuse your powers," Kanvar shouted. "Your actions are unbecoming of a king. The Great Blue dragons are free and have been since the fall of Stonefountain. They won't be enslaved again now."

*You think you can stop me? Your powers are no match for mine.* Rajahansa wrapped his power around Kanvar and sent a jolt like a bolt of lightning into his mind.

Kanvar cried out, tore the lid off the cookpot, and lifted Akshara's singing stone from its iron prison. "I summon Akshara from the grave. Let the Great Blue Liberator punish you for your crimes here today." The pain of the singing stone was every bit as intense to Kanvar's mind as Rajahansa's blow had been, but the stone affected Rajahansa and his cohorts as well as Kanvar.

The Great Gold dragons roared in pain and took a step back. Haidar and Liander pressed their hands against their heads.

The singing stone broke Rajahansa's hold over the Great Blue dragons. Anilon leaped to his feet, howled in fury, and launched himself at Rajahansa.

His claws tore into Rajahansa's chest, and his jaws closed over his throat so a single shake of his head would tear it out.

Rajahansa let out a desperate puff of joy breathe. The glittering breath settled onto Anilon's face. Anilon's jaws relaxed and he slumped to the ground, crooning happily.

Panting and bleeding, Rajahansa stepped away from him, then realized the entire Great Blue dragon pride was advancing on him. Even with the help of the other two gold dragons, they couldn't breathe joy breathe enough to stop all of the blues.

Rajahansa jumped into the air and rushed away, followed by the other dragons and their Nagas.

The Great Blue dragons swarmed into the air after them, intent on shredding their prey.

"Wait! Come back!" Kanvar yelled. "Stay within range of the singing stone."

Only the oldest and slowest heard him. The ancient blue pivoted in the sky and dove back to Kanvar.

"Warn the others," Kanvar said. "I can't speak to their minds while holding the stone. But you can. Call them back. If they get too far away, Rajahansa will take control of them again."

The dragon nodded and a few moments later the rest of the Great Blue dragon pride returned to the meadow.

They eyed Elkatran like he was next on their list for destruction.

"No, don't," Kanvar said. "Elkatran is a friend. He came here with me to save you. He defied his own father in your behalf."

The Great Blue dragons growled but didn't attack.

Groaning, Anilon shook off the effects of the joy breath and lumbered to his feet. He stalked over to Kanvar. His dragonstone flashed.

"I'm sorry, I can't hear you," Kanvar said, holding up Akshara's stone, "not while I have this out."

Anilon held out a foreclaw to Kanvar.

"I agree," Kanvar said. "This singing stone belongs in possession of the Great Blue dragon pride. Since you are its leader now, I give the stone to you." Kanvar held out the stone, and Anilon took it from the small human hand into his own giant claw and nodded thanks.

As soon as Anilon had the stone, Elkatran took to the air and rushed from the nesting grounds, getting as far away as he could from the angry blue dragons. When the cry of the singing stone no longer encompassed them, Elkatran heaved a sigh of relief. *I thought they were going to tear me to shreds. That's what we get for helping them, I suppose. The Great Blue dragons never had any bit of decency to them.*

Kanvar grunted in amusement. *I wish we could have kept the stone, but it is theirs. If I had not taken it with me, they would never have been in danger from* Rajahansa.

*I wish we could have kept it though. Without it, how will we free your father? Rajahansa is too powerful for either of us.*

*He's not too powerful for Dharanidhar.*

*If Dharanidhar were at his full power and Haidar and Liander weren't helping Rajahansa.*

Kanvar gritted his teeth. The high wind skimmed his cheeks and flapped through his hair as the mountains fell away behind him. *Just take me to Dharanidhar. Tell Devaj and Bensharie to meet us there as soon as Bensharie has rested enough to make the flight. We will find a way to save my father.*

**Rajan watched the streak** of sunlight from the window-slit above his head move across the floor as the sun crossed the sky. Garron had left his hands bound and shoved him into a narrow room. It was bare and cold and wet. The paleness of the white limestone floor and walls grated on Rajan's nerves. The only relief from the bland whiteness was a barred window in the door, which gave view to a blank white hall beyond. Cold water dripped from the limestone, smelling like ocean salt, and Rajan realized the whole ground floor of the palace must have flooded when the great wave hit, driving a wall of water up the river to where the castle stood on the bank.

"I really hate this palace." Rajan leaned his head back against the wall and stretched his feet out in front of him.

Vitra had promised torture and delivered it in the form of cold white nothingness. When Rajan started shivering, he imagined himself in his red dragon form, slipping into the luxurious, rich heat of the magma pool in his lair. Fire and heat and burning rock. The memory did not stop his teeth from chattering.

Soft footsteps outside snagged his attention. He sat up straighter and gazed through the window in the door. There was a rustle of clothing and then the face of a young boy peeked through the bars. His pale blue eyes were set in a delicate face, his hair was so blond it was almost white, or was that just the whiteness of the walls reflecting off of it?

The boy looked at Rajan for a moment, then blinked and sighed as if disappointed.

"What's wrong?" Rajan said. "Am I not who you were looking for?"

"Not what I expected." The boy gripped the bars with pale fingers.

"What . . . did you expect?"

"I heard the men talking. They said there was a Great Red volcanic dragon locked up in here."

Rajan choked back a laugh. "If there was, it would have to be a very small dragon. A wyrmling, and it would be freezing its scaly little hide off. Red dragons prefer warm places like volcanoes."

"I don't think it's cold in here?" The boy's voice took on a sassy tone.

"Because you're wearing a shirt, no doubt," Rajan said.

"Of course I'm wearing a shirt. Why aren't you?" The boy pressed his face closer to the bars.

"Because I'm a red dragon, and dragons don't wear shirts. But they do eat little boys." Rajan snapped his teeth, and the boy jumped back.

"Now run along back to some part of the castle where it's safe," Rajan said.

A look of sadness swept across the boy's face. "I don't think anywhere is safe anymore. Not since the ground started shaking and the walls fell down."

Remembering what Theodoric had said about the children being buried in the rubble, Rajan didn't know how to respond. He'd seldom known a safe moment in his life since he'd come down with the dragon fever.

"Shaunty?" Theodoric's voice echoed down the hall.

The boy jumped in surprise and stepped away from the grate.

Theodoric walked up and grabbed his arm. "Why is it I always find you every place you're not supposed to be?"

"I wanted to see the red dragon," Shaunty squeaked.

"The red dragon, what?" Theodoric said.

Rajan cleared his throat.

Theodoric glanced through the grate and frowned. "Come along. There's no red dragon here."

"No, wait." Shaunty slipped out of his father's grasp. "Captain Vitra said you were going to kill him, but he's not a dragon. He's a man. Why must you kill him?"

Theodoric flashed a glare at Rajan and knelt down to talk to Shaunty at eye level. "It's the law, son. A law given to us long ago by the Naga kings of Stonefountain who we've sworn to serve. We can't break that law."

"Why not?" Shaunty glanced to Rajan then back to his father.

"Because if we don't follow the laws, terrible things can happen." Theodoric's solemn voice brooked no more argument.

Shaunty blinked back sudden tears. "Terrible things have already happened. What law did we break? Why is my sister dead?"

"Shaunty." Theodoric scooped the boy up in his arms and strode away. *I will deal with you later*, he shot into Rajan's mind along with a sudden rush of anger as if the earthquake and the great wave were all Rajan's fault.

*Don't hurry on my account,* Rajan responded. *I'm not going anywhere. Though I might die from the cold before you get around to killing me.*

Lord Theodoric slammed a wall up between their minds, cutting Rajan off.

Rajan gritted his teeth. Lord Theodoric's daughter dead from the earthquake. Naga children buried in the rubble. No wonder the Nagas had been slow to respond to the wider catastrophe throughout the city.

**The sun set and** rose again before Garron came for Rajan. He opened the door and ordered Rajan to his feet.

Rajan complied, reminding himself that he'd agreed to this in exchange for Kumar's life. In the back of his mind, he could feel Kumar alive and awake somewhere out in the city, but he could not see into Kumar's thoughts. Kumar had put up a shield so no Nagas could tell what he was doing. Rajan wasn't sure if he should be concerned about what his brother was up to or not.

Garron forced him up the stairs and through halls scattered with broken stones and dust. The quake had taken its toll on the palace. They came to a set of double doors, inlaid with golden images of Stonefountain. Garron thrust the doors open and pushed Rajan inside.

Beyond the doors, a great hall stretched up to a dais topped with a golden throne. Light from a row of shattered stained-glass windows illuminated the room. Only one window remained intact, the one at the head of the hall overlooking Lord Theodoric on the throne. His Lordship was now cleaned up, shaved, and dressed in heavy golden robes. He looked tired, spent of physical energy and emotional strength. Men and women in flowing robes and fine dresses lined either side of the hall, leaving an aisle open for Garron to drag Rajan to the foot of the dais and force him to his knees. Rajan was surprised to realize that most of the people's minds were shielded from him. So many Nagas gathered in one place.

Theodoric shifted in his throne and looked down on Rajan with distaste. "Well, renegade. It has come to my attention that you claim to be from the Western world. Is that true?"

"Yes, My Lord. I was born in Daro, a city on the northern coast of Varna."

"Varna? I have not heard that name."

"The continent where the ruins of Stonefountain can be found. You do realize that Stonefountain was overthrown a thousand years ago?" Rajan didn't want to be the bearer of that news if they hadn't heard it, but he couldn't see how he could avoid it.

"We know what happened at Stonefountain," Theodoric snapped.

Rajan pressed his lips together and fell silent.

"We have not heard any news from the Western world in my lifetime. There is much I need to know. You will answer my questions," Theodoric said.

"Why should I?" Rajan said. "You're going to kill me anyway. Besides, what do you care about the other side of the world? If you really wanted information, you could have flown over there and gotten it yourself."

Lord Theodoric jumped to his feet. "My father sent men to bring back news. None of them returned. I sent my oldest son. He did not return. I demand to know what became of him."

"He's dead, I'm sure. They all are because Nagas are killed on sight there, or murdered before they are old enough to bond. The humans hate Nagas, and Akshara found the means to destroy them. Few ever escape that destiny."

"You did." Theodoric took a step down toward him. Grief overshadowed his eyes as if news that his oldest son was dead only compounded the loss of his daughter.

"I wish I hadn't. I can't tell you how many times I've cursed my father's crossbow bolt for not taking me in the heart. A swift death would have been better than the life I've lived." Rajan shuddered.

A murmur swept through the crowd of Nagas.

"Your father . . . shot you?" Theodoric's fists clenched.

"Of course he did, because if anyone found out he had a Naga son, he and his entire family would be slaughtered: men, women, children, grandparents, aunts, uncles, cousins. The humans will not risk even one Naga being born and coming to power. They seek the eradication of all Naga bloodlines." Rajan clenched his teeth and fell silent. He'd said enough. Too much probably, considering he'd so recently almost succeeded in taking over the Western world.

Theodoric shook his head as if it were a nightmare too horrible to consider. He returned to his throne, frowning.

Captain Vitra stepped forward. "Where he's from does not matter. Our laws are clear, and since this is the last bastion of civilization, it seems, we are bound to follow them. He bonded with a dragon other than a Great Gold chosen by you; his life is forfeit. We cannot have renegade Nagas polluting the bloodlines and vying for power against the golden throne."

Rajan bowed his head. *Silverwave, I'm sorry.* He felt her, still out by the reef, weeping.

"Yet I wonder," Lord Theodoric said softly, "if he had been here with us, if he would not have followed our laws? If I had chosen a Great Gold companion for him, would he have accepted that bond? What say you, renegade?"

Rajan remained speechless. The thought that his life might have been so blessed by the fountain that he could have bonded with a Great Gold dragon and lived in the luxury of this palace was beyond his ability to imagine.

"Speak," Theodoric said. "Will you give no defense for yourself?"

Rajan glanced at Captain Vitra and shook his head. He'd sworn by Stonefountain to accept execution if Vitra's dragon healed Kumar. Clearly Vitra felt him honor-bound to follow through with that oath.

"Captain Vitra is right. I accept your law and await execution." Rajan bowed his head and took a shuddering breath.

"Vitra," Theodoric said sharply. "Have you twisted his mind to accept this conviction?"

"Of course not," Vitra said.

Rajan's skin prickled. "He has not, My Lord."

Lord Theodoric sucked in a pained breath. "Then I have no choice. I sentence you to death by beheading. Captain Vitra—"

A crash and splintering of glass cut off Lord Theodoric's command.

Rajan snapped up his head and saw that a heavy crossbow bolt had smashed through the stained-glass window overlooking the dais and embedded itself in the throne. A rope had been tied to the bolt, and a figure clad in red dragonscale armor, carrying a pole with one of the palace's golden Stonefountain flags, hauled itself in through the window. Kumar Raza stepped onto the dais and planted the flag beside him.

"You fly the flag of Stonefountain, and I'm told you swear fealty to the golden throne. Is that true? Or have you forsaken all oaths to your king?" Kumar said, leveling a glare at Captain Vitra who had his sword raised over Rajan's neck.

The gathered Nagas shuffled back in surprise except for those in the uniform of the Naga Gaurd who drew their swords and rushed onto the dais, placing themselves between Kumar and Lord Theodoric.

"If there were a king still sitting on the throne of Stonefountain, we would follow his command, of course," Theodoric said. "I and my fathers before me have never betrayed the royal trust or broken the law."

"Very well then," Kumar said. "I call on you to deliver this renegade to His Majasty Amar, grandson of Khalid, the Naga King, for judgment."

Theodoric pointed an angry finger at Kumar. "The royal family perished a thousand years ago."

Kumar shook his head. "King Khalid's youngest son was carried to safety in Kundiland. Though he was later murdered by Naga hunters, his son survived him and ascended to the throne. I should know. I am His Majesty's father-in-law and closest friend. And I assure you, he won't be happy if you execute his wife's uncle."

Rajan grinned at the pallor that spread across Lord Theodoric's face.

"You have no proof of this," Captain Vitra shouted. "You are making up stories in a foolish attempt to save your brother's life."

"You two are brothers?" Lord Theodoric said, glancing from Rajan to Kumar and back.

"Twins," Kumar said. "Though how he got to be a Naga and I didn't, I'll never know. It doesn't seem fair."

"He's lying. Kill him," Captain Vitra ordered his men. They rushed at Kumar. Rajan expected Kumar to draw his sword and defend himself, but Kumar just laughed and ducked the first sword strike, blocked the second with the flag pole, and sidestepped the third.

"Come now, My Lord," Kumar said. "You're a Naga. You can see for yourself if I'm lying or not. My mind is open to you."

"Hold!" Theodoric shouted. The Naga Guard backed away from Kumar.

Lord Theodoric locked eyes with Kumar and stared in silence for an uncomfortable length of time. Finally, he looked away and wiped a bead of sweat from his forehead. "He speaks the truth," he said to the crowd. "There is a royal heir. Put your swords away, all of you." He pointed at Rajan. "This man will go to the king for judgment."

## Chapter Thirteen

**Elkatran landed on the** sandy beach of the cove and helped Kanvar from his back. Kanvar thanked him and limped toward the cave where Dharanidhar awaited his arrival. The setting sun lit the water with gold. The jungle heat drenched Kanvar with sweat. A pack of black monkeys hopped around in the tree branches and filled the air with their screams. Kanvar sucked in the sounds and smells of jungle heat and home.

Elkatran curled up on the sand and tried not to think how close he had come to being shredded by furious Great Blue dragons. His mind was troubled about Rajahansa's actions and just as worried about Devaj. Since the encounter with Khalid at Stonefountain, Devaj had kept his mind locked away from Elkatran. To protect Elkatran from the pain, no doubt. But Elkatran didn't like it.

*When you've rested, will you go hunt something for Dharanidhar to eat?* Kanvar asked him.

Elkatran recoiled. He was hungry himself. He hadn't eaten much since he and Devaj had left the castle. Kanvar realized that, as Rajahansa's son, Elkatran had never in his life hunted for food. Someone else raised the animals he fed on, slaughtered them, and cooked them for him. The idea of killing some lesser creature, cleaning and skinning it, and cooking it to eat was abhorrent to him.

Kanvar shook his head in frustration. *So you're just going to starve to death?*

*I think maybe I'll try eating plants. I'm sure there must be many edible plants in the jungle.* Elkatran looked longingly at the vegetation. *Humans eat plants. I should be able to eat plants too.*

A rumble of laughter rolled from the cave. *Gold dragons*, Dharanidhar muttered in amusement.

Kanvar was too frustrated to be amused. He'd risked everything, including his own life to save the humans from Rajan and the Great Red dragon. And the only thanks he got for it was the humans banding together to hunt him and his family, and the other Nagas turning against him and his dragon. His arriving in the nick of time to save the Great Blue dragons from slavery had not regained Dharanidhar's and his acceptance back into the pride.

Ignoring the fancy arches carved into the stone at the entrance of the cave, Kanvar stalked into Akshara's lair. Dharanidhar lay near the back, gaunt, old and scarred.

*You should have let me fly you up to the pride*, Dharanidhar said. *I would have finished Rajahansa for you.*

"And killed my father? No, don't even start, Dharanidhar, I don't want to argue with you. Just help me think of some way to get my father away from Rajahansa. I can't believe he would use his joy breath on his own Naga and chain him up. How could he? Why would he?"

*You don't want me to answer that, since you just claimed you don't want to argue with me*, Dharanidhar growled.

"Fine. Rajahansa has turned evil. There, I said it. Are you happy?"

*Rajahansa was always power hungry and domineering. You just didn't want to see it.*

"We have seen into my father's mind, down to the deepest layers, to his very heart. You and I both know my father is not like that." Kanvar limped over to Dharanidhar and rubbed the smooth cold scales on his foreleg.

*I have seen your father's heart, and he is a good man, but just because the Naga is good, doesn't mean the dragon he's bound to will be.* Dharanidhar rose and stretched.

"But I never felt such evil from Rajahansa's mind before."

*No? What about when Indumauli first told you about him, claiming that the Great Gold dragon king would hang his hide on the wall if he bonded with you? What about when your father first plucked you from the ledge above the jungle village? It was Rajahansa who ordered him to bind your body and mind so you could not resist them. Think back, Kanvar, every encounter you've had with Rajahansa, has he ever been kind, gentle, caring? No. Do not confuse your father with Rajahansa.*

"But they are bound together. One mind, one being."

*Not any more than you and I are. And we certainly disagree often enough.*

"But my father should have been able to stop him from enslaving the Great Blue dragons."

*Of course he should have, Kanvar, but he obviously didn't. Rajahansa is stronger than your father, it seems.*

"No. If Rajahansa could control my father, he would not have had to chain him. My father is good, and he's resisting Rajahansa's evils. Get up. We need to hunt some food so you'll have enough strength to fly me to the palace to save him."

*Then Rajahansa and I will confront each other.*

"I suppose that's inevitable." Kanvar's irritation had only increased while talking to Dharanidhar. "So get up."

*I will, but you need to go gather some vines. I'm afraid there wasn't time to get your saddle on my neck before I had to leave the palace.*

"Why didn't you say that while I was still outside?" Gritting his teeth, Kanvar drew his father's sword and limped back out into the darkness.

**Rajan stood in a** palace room and watched hot water stream from a fixture in the wall into a large marble tub.

"What I don't get, is how they got the water in the wall in the first place, let alone how it could be hot."

Kumar laughed. "That's how I felt when I first saw something like this at the golden palace in Kundiland. Wonderful, isn't it? And when you're done with the bath, you just pull the plug there in the bottom of the tub and the water drains right out."

"Won't that make a mess on the floor."

"No. It goes into the pipes." Kumar handed Rajan a wash cloth and bar of sweet-scented soap.

"Pipes?"

"Round metal tubes. Listen, Rajan, don't question it. Just enjoy it."

Rajan rubbed his sore wrists where the rope had bound his hands. His whole body was scratched and bruised. The wounds from the redwings had healed, thanks to Vitra's reluctant dragon. But Rajan was covered with crusted blood and stunk worse than camdor droppings. He stepped into the tub and let his body slide into the warm water.

"I had a pool like this back in the volcano." He wet his face and scrubbed his fingers through his hair. "Without the magic water spout and drain, of course. Ah, to be warm again. I was afraid I never would be."

"You what?" Kumar clenched his fist and stepped toward him. Rajan remembered too late that his brother thought Kanvar had erased his memories.

Rajan raised a placating hand. "It's not Kanvar's fault. He didn't have time to erase my memories. He locked them up instead, behind a wall that I couldn't get through. But I got hit on the head, hard, by the boat when the great wave caught us. It shattered the wall, and I . . . almost ate a baby, but I didn't. All right. I didn't hurt anyone. I tried to save the people trapped in the rubble instead. I know you don't want me to remember everything I did, but I can't help it. It's a part of me. I can't change that."

Red seeped up Kumar's neck and across his face.

"Don't be angry, please."

Kumar frowned and left the room without speaking.

Rajan scrubbed himself clean and climbed out of the water reluctantly, stepping from the bathing room into a larger room equipped with a fluffy goose down mattress laid out on a white limestone frame carved in the shape of a flying dragon. The whole room spoke of lavishness. From the elegant tapestries on the wall, to the gold-inlaid wardrobe and writing desk, to the mirror and washstand set with brushes, combs, and shaving blade. A window on the far wall looked out over the river several stories below.

Kumar sat on the bed polishing his sword. A frown still creased his forehead. Rajan could not read Kumar's mind through his brother's shields, but he feared Kumar would despise him for his time with the red dragon.

"Don't hate me," Rajan said. "I'm trying to be better. To be different. I'm sorry the red dragon had to come between us."

Kumar dropped his sword, and it clattered against the polished white limestone. His eyes flashed to Rajan's face. "I don't hate you. Of course, I don't hate you. Why would you think that?"

"You are very angry at Kanvar. You wanted him to make me a good person, and he didn't." Rajan dropped his gaze to his feet and clenched his fists. He even hated himself.

"No." Kumar rose to his feet. "It was never about making you a good person. It was about keeping you from suffering any more than you already have. The red dragon hurt you, and I didn't want you to go on hurting. I thought if the memories were gone, you would be happier."

"I wasn't happy without my memories. I was lost, confused, empty. All I knew was my old life, and you told me I couldn't have that, but you wouldn't tell me why. I just wanted to go home to Daro because that was all I knew." Rajan let out a bitter laugh. "Daro . . . you're right. I can't go back there. They would kill me. For one small moment I had the whole world in my hands. Everyone under my control. Their minds, their hearts, their souls belonged to me." The feeling of power and exaltation would never leave him.

Kumar snorted. "Under the red dragon's control, you mean. You didn't even have power over yourself."

"Well, now I do. Can't you accept that . . . can't you accept me for what I am, not some idealized childhood memory from your own mind?"

The room fell silent. Kumar lifted his sword from the floor and sheathed it then put away his whetstone and polishing cloth. "You are my brother, Rajan. You can always count on me to accept you even if the rest of the world won't."

Rajan let out a relieved breath.

"I found some clothes in the wardrobe and laid them out for you." Kumar pointed to a pair of underclothes, black trousers, white silk shirt, and red vest on the bed.

"You expect me to wear those?" Rajan said. "I'll look like one of those pompous Naga Guardsmen."

"They wear gold, not red." Kumar unbuckled his armor. "What are you complaining about anyway? You're lucky to be alive. Does it really matter what you wear?"

"All right. Fine. Thank you. I did say thank you for saving my life twice already, you know."

"I know." Kumar grinned and headed for the bathing room.

"But seriously, you had to come through the window? Couldn't you have just used the door like a normal person?" Rajan snatched up the shirt and slid it on over his head. The silk settled cool and luxurious against his skin.

Kumar snorted. "One thing I learned long ago. Nobody listens to normal people. I had to get His Lordship's attention."

“It doesn’t seem fair that the window should survive the earthquake and be shattered by you.”

“You’re just jealous because you didn’t think of telling Lord Theodoric you were related to King Amar. You don’t know His Majesty like I do.”

“And what is His Majesty going to do with me once Lord Theodoric turns me over to him?”

“He’ll give you a big hug, welcome you to the palace, and serve you dinner.”

That didn’t seem likely. “What about the laws about only bonding with a Great Gold dragon.”

“He let Kanvar live, and Kanvar bonded with the Great Gold dragon king’s worst enemy. Plus Kanvar’s a cripple. Khalid would have had him killed at birth. The old laws mean nothing to Amar. He cares only for the well-being of his family and other Nagas who have survived. Besides, how is Lord Theodoric going to turn you over to him? It’s not like he’s going to leave his fancy palace and his great kingdom and fly to the other side of the world. Don’t worry, Rajan. Come morning we’ll be on our way.”

“I have friends in this city who need help. I can’t just—”

Kumar stepped into the bathing room and closed the door behind him.

Rajan got the rest of his clothes on and set about trying to untangle his hair and shave his scraggly beard. A light knock at the door stopped him mid-shave.

"Come in," he said hesitantly.

The door opened a crack and Lord Theodoric slipped into the room. "I hope you find these accommodations hospitable."

Rajan stared at him unspeaking, the razor blade clutched motionless in his hand.

Theodoric frowned at Rajan's silence. "Is the room to your liking?"

"Oh." Rajan shook himself. "Yes. Thank you. Much better than the last accommodation you gave me. Are you trying to be friendly now?"

Theodoric glanced around the room. "Where's your brother?"

Rajan pointed the razor toward the bathing room.

"I wanted to speak with him."

"Of course." Rajan went back to shaving, his nerves taut, not knowing if Lord Theodoric was friend or foe at the moment.

Theodoric pulled the chair out from the writing desk and sat down. Through the silence they could hear water splash in the tub from the next room.

Rajan wiped the foam from the blade and started on the next section of his face. "I'm sorry about your daughter . . . and your son."

Theodoric made a faint noise at the back of his throat but said nothing.

Rajan was relieved when Kumar stepped back into the

room. Dripping wet, he went to the wardrobe and pulled out some underclothes for himself. "Did you polish my armor, little brother?"

Rajan set down the razor blade and wiped the last of the soap from his face. "Polish your own fancypants armor."

Kumar laughed and swung around to face Rajan while he pulled on a pair of green chausses he'd grabbed out of the wardrobe.

Rajan pointed to Lord Theodoric, sitting by the writing desk.

Kumar choked, swiped a shirt from the wardrobe and got it on followed by a green tunic. "Forgive me, My Lord. I did not realize you were there."

Lord Theodoric stood. "Welcome to Aesir, capital of Navgarod. I hope you will excuse these humble accommodations, but we are laboring under some difficulty at the moment. I hope His Majesty will not be angry at my negligence on your behalf."

"Humble accommodations?" Rajan blurted out. He'd never even dreamed a place like this could exist. "What's the matter with you? Have you no sense of reality? Thousands of people in the outer city have no roof over their head at all. Supplies from this one room could give comfort to a dozen families. You can't just stand here and let them go hungry and cold."

Kumar stepped in front of Rajan and edged his brother away from Lord Theodoric. "These chambers are comfortable enough and greatly appreciated. And I'm sure you and your men are doing everything they can for the welfare of your people."

"Supplies have started arriving from the outer provinces." Theodoric smoothed his robes. "Soon the suffering will be alleviated for everyone. Despite what you think, I am aware of the wellbeing of every person in this city. I have attuned my mind to the citizens under my protection. Admittedly, I blocked them all out while I attended to the needs of the children here at the palace, but what man wouldn't see to his own family first?"

"Wait, you—" Rajan's throat tightened as he tried to speak. The immensity of what Theodoric suggested staggered him.

"I feel their pain, and their sorrow. It is my duty as Lord."

Rajan backed away and leaned against the wall, pressing his hands to his head. How often had he blocked out the suffering of the red dragon's human captives? How hard had he tried to do the same here, shielding his sense of self from the humans in the city that first night when he realized he could not save them all?

"You're young." Theodoric walked around Kumar to stand in front of Rajan. "Someone your age could not begin to take on such a responsibility, especially without training. Give yourself time. A Naga's power grows with age."

Somehow that did not make Rajan feel any better.

"Is there something you wanted?" Kumar picked up a comb and ran it through his beard. Gray streaked his red-gold hair.

"Yes, please forgive me." Theodoric turned his attention back to Kumar Raza. "Something I saw in your mind is bothering me."

"Only one thing? Because right now I have a lot of things that are bothering me." Kumar finished with his hair and looked over at his armor as if anxious to set about cleaning it.

"Kanvar said that the combined human armies know where His Majesty is and are sailing there to destroy him." Theodoric's hand strayed to the sword belted at his waist.

"Yes. That is high on my list of concerns," Kumar said. "Which is why I must ask your leave first thing in the morning. His Majesty knows nothing of armies and fighting. I must return and help him."

"His Majesty has no army to protect him?"

"No. We're going to have to find a new place to hide. It means he will have to leave behind his palace in Kundiland, but we can rebuild. There are so few Nagas left alive, keeping them that way has to be the highest priority."

"And the humans have singing stones so he can't just take control of their minds?" Theodoric said, a frown creasing his face.

"Yes," Kumar said.

Rajan shuddered. He never wanted to be around a singing stone again.

Theodoric nodded, paced across the room and back to Kumar. He drew his sword and watched the light glint off the steel blade. "Since the fall of Stonefountain, the Naga Guard has trained to fight like human men, knowing they can't always count on their powers to protect them. My men and their dragons will not be paralyzed by the singing stones. Long we have trained and waited, knowing someday we might be called upon to battle the humans. Now we have word that a king survives. It is our duty to hasten to his defense. Tomorrow, I'll leave Navgarod under Garron's command and lead my men across the ocean to the Western world. You will guide us to His Majesty's side."

Rajan's mind buzzed with surprise. He had no desire to travel with Theodoric and his Nagas.

Kumar raked his fingers through his beard. "I think it would make more sense for me to return to Kundiland alone and guide His Majesty here. The humans have lost all record of this land. They believe if they sail too far they will fall of the end of the world. Bringing His Majesty and his family here is the safest course."

Lord Theodoric slammed his sword back into its sheath. "The decision is not yours. I will take my men to Kundiland and the king will decide if we stand and fight or retreat to these walls."

## Chapter Fourteen

**Rajan picked at the** feast that had been left for him in his room: roast bovinder, flayed dragonfish, steaming vegetables and a sugar-coated fruit he'd never seen before. Kumar had spent the day helping Lord Theodoric plan and prepare for the Naga Guard to fly to Kundiland. Rajan had eaten his fill but there was so much food spread out on the desk that it made him crazy just letting it sit when he knew Dove, her daughter, and the other survivors were out in a ruined city, cold and hungry.

He threw down his fork and went to the door, intent on finding Kumar and Theodoric and demanding they let him take the rest of the food to his friends. But when he opened the door, two of the Naga Guard who had been standing outside drew their swords and barred his way.

"Let me pass," Rajan said.

"You are still in His Lordship's custody until he hands you over to the king for judgment and execution," one of the guards snapped. "This room may be nicer than the one Garron gave you previously, but for you it is still a prison."

Rajan slammed the door in the guards' faces and went to the cleaned and polished stack of Kumar's armor and weapons. He buckled on the sword, calculating his chances of defeating both opponents at the door. He was good, but would not be able to silence them with the sword before they could shout for help.

He picked up Kumar's crossbow and loaded it.

*What are you doing?* Silverwave asked.

He jumped in surprise and almost dropped the crossbow. He hadn't realized she had left the reef and swum up the river toward him.

*What are the odds this king will execute me? Kumar doesn't think he will, but the Nagas do.*

*Does it matter? You gave yourself up for execution.*

*Yes, and they had the chance to kill me and didn't. I figure I've more than fulfilled my part of the bargain in that. And I've been thinking. Do we really want a Naga king in the world again? Kumar thinks he's a nice guy, but how can he be? A descendant of Khalid? Maybe he's nice now, with the singing stones to negate his power, with no army. How many Nagas are in the Guard? I'm guessing at least fifty. But maybe three times that. You know how much damage I did in Maran by myself. Imagine an army of Nagas loose in the world.* Goose-bumps broke out on Rajan's arms. *I don't understand why Kumar isn't trying to stop them.*

*He can't. If he acts like anything other than an ally, they'll kill you both. Your power can't match theirs, and for all his fighting ability, he can't outfight a whole army. He's chosen the wiser course, trusting that King Amar will keep the Naga Guard under control once they reach Kundiland. You should sit tight and trust your brother to handle this.*

Rajan paced across the room, kicked the wardrobe, and paced back. He rubbed his chest where Dove had leaned up against him, and imagined her daughter's warm body snuggled in his arms. *Silverwave, I have to go to them. Lord Theodoric will take me away in the morning, and I will never get to see them again. I have to at least say goodbye.*

He picked up the crossbow and went to the door.

*Don't.*

He could feel Silverwave snaking through the water below. She shared a better idea with him.

He set the crossbow back down next to Kumar's armor and returned to the wardrobe, going through its contents until he found a hooded cloak. He wrapped all the food up in the cloak, set that on the bed, rolled all the bedding up around it, and tied the bundle with cord from one of the tapestries.

He lifted the bundle onto his shoulder and went to the window. There had once been a pane of glass there, but like so many in the grand hall, it had shattered and been cleared away. Below him swirled the wide river waters.

*Ready?* he asked Silverwave.

*Yes.*

*You won't drop me?*

*I might.* Silverwave laughed at him.

Grinning, Rajan climbed up onto the windowsill and then jumped as far out over the water as he could. And he fell, wind whistling past his ears, trying to tear the bundle from his hands.

When he was halfway down, Silverwave leaped from the water below, caught him, spread her wing fins, and glided to land gently on the riverbank.

"Thank you." Rajan rubbed her cool damp scales. "Meet me at the dock closest to the outer city."

*There's nothing left of the docks, but I'll meet you there. Now hurry. Who knows how long before they discover you are missing.*

Rajan sucked in a breath and bolted toward the outer city. He ran hard, sending his thoughts out in front of him to sense where the city watch were and avoid them. If death was the penalty for looting an average home, he didn't want to imagine what the penalty would be for looting the palace. The thought made him chuckle. He would have burst out into a full laugh, if all his breath wasn't being used to run.

He wasn't sure how long it would take him to get across the city, but he glanced at the sky often in search of the gold dragons. He had no doubt they would come after him.

# Dragonbound V

**Kumar Raza surveyed the** stripped bed and empty room.

"Where is he?" Theodoric demanded. "How could he have gone anywhere? The guards swear they didn't let him out the door."

Kumar noted the missing sword and the loaded crossbow. "He said he had friends in the city." He crossed to the window and looked down to the black water below.

"I told him they would be cared for. He didn't need to take any of this." Red tinged Theodoric's cheeks, but he looked more puzzled than angry.

"There was a woman."

"Ah . . ."

"A woman. And we are leaving in the morning." Kumar choked back a laugh. "I can't tell you how happy it makes me to think that someone has stirred a bit of humanity in him. When Kanvar and I found him, his sense of identity was only red dragon." Kumar rubbed the bite scar on his face. "What does it matter where he spends the night? You can always pick him up again in the morning. He can't hide from you, can he? You said you can sense everyone in the city."

"I can, and he's out there, though he has his mind shielded from me. I'm sure I could find him. But how did he escape?"

"The window." Kumar sat on the bed and pulled off his boots.

"It's too small for a dragon to fly through."

"He jumped."

Theodoric crossed the room and leaned out the window. "That's still too far a drop, even into water."

"Great Silver serpents can jump quite high and fly for short distances. She caught him. I've seen her do it before, when he fell from higher up than this."

"All right. I'll give your brother one night with his woman. Then if he tries to escape again, I'll put him in chains." Theodoric slapped the windowsill then strode out of the room.

Kumar heaved a sigh of relief. He opened his mind to the bond he shared with his twin. He could not send his thoughts like a Naga, but if Rajan noticed him and listened, he would hear. *Run fast, little brother, if escape is what you want. You have until morning to be long gone from this city.*

*Kumar?*

*If you're just saying goodbye to your friends, I'll see you in the morning.*

**Rajan halted as his** brother's thoughts lilted through his mind and vanish as Kumar raised shields around his own mind so the Nagas would not know he'd talked to Rajan.

Rajan shivered and forced himself to get moving again. He was too tired to run anymore. He'd passed through the ring of mansions and the streets of stone houses. The poorer wood-framed houses were severely damaged. Beyond them lay the rubble of the outer city and the flickering fires of the survivor camp. He'd avoided the city watch and seen no sign of the Naga Guard, but he'd had to use his powers on a number of people who saw what he carried and wanted to take it from him. He feared Theodoric or Vitra would sense his use of power and come for him.

The night chill seeped in through his silk shirt as he crossed to the outer city and picked his way through the rubble. As he grew closer, he realized the survivor camp had spread and grown. In the time he'd been gone, the people had cobbled together sticks and cloth to make tent shelters. The overwhelming scent of death still smothered all else.

"Hold there," a grim voice ordered as he came to the edge of camp. "Speak your name. What business do you have here?"

"Rajan. I need to speak with Frederick and Dove."

"Rajan? Never heard of you."

Great. A new person who did not know him. He thought about explaining, but shrugged it off as too complicated. "Let me pass," he ordered.

The man's mind bent to his will, and he said nothing as Rajan hurried by. Rajan opened his mind up to the people around him, searching for Dove's. Hunger and sorrow washed over him. Theodoric's aid had not yet begun to reach the outer city, and Rajan doubted it ever would. He had to be careful then. Hundreds of hungry people would love to tear the bundle from his shoulder and use it for themselves. He wished he had enough food for everyone. If only there were some way to force the Nagas to share more of their own supplies, but Rajan had been lucky to escape with his life.

He found Frederick first, sitting next to a fire, tending Henry's wounds.

"Henry." Rajan set down the bundle and knelt next to his friend, the one man who had stood with him against the redwings. "You're alive. Thank the fountain. I feared they'd kill you. I tried to stop them."

Henry groaned and looked up into Rajan's face. "I feared the same of you when the whole swarm came after you. How did you survive?"

"The Naga Guard killed the redwings and took me to the palace for judgment and execution." Rajan lifted his hands to the fire, enjoying its warmth.

"Some kind of execution, do they always dress renegade Nagas up so royally before they kill them?" Frederick said.

Rajan ran his hand down the smooth sleeve of the silk shirt and fingered the stitching on the vest. "No. The clothes came later."

Rajan explained to Henry and Frederick about what had happened at the palace.

"Your brother's alive then, and can walk?" Frederick said. "Too bad the Nagas don't share the dragon saliva with the rest of us."

"I suppose he's in trouble now that I've run away," Rajan said. "But I have to see Dove. I need to know she and her daughter will be all right. Where is she?"

Frederick pointed to a ragged tent off in the darkness.

"Thank you." Rajan took up his bundle and made his way past several sleeping families before curling his fingers around the edge of the mud-splattered rug that hung over a few pieces of wood tied together with twine.

"Dove," he whispered. "May I come in?"

There was a faint rustle behind the rug and a moan.

"Dove?" Rajan had to get on his hands and knees to crawl into the tiny enclosure. Inside was dark, and he wished for a torch or a candle so he could see. Should have thought to loot those from the palace as well.

"Dove, are you in here?" he felt across the ground in front of him, and his fingers found her leg and thigh. She had curled into a ball with Eleanor in her arms, and was shivering.

"Please, leave me alone. I don't have anything." Her voice was faint.

"Dove. It's Rajan. I'm not going to hurt you." He unrolled the bedding and set aside the cloak and food, then wrapped the warm sheets and blankets over her.

"Da?" Eleanor said. Tiny hands reached from beneath the blankets to rub his face.

Rajan took the little hands in his own and kissed them. “I’m not really your father, little one, but you can call me that if you wish.”

“Rajan.” Dove wrapped her arms around him and pressed a face wet with tears against his neck. “I thought you were dead. The redwings, I thought they’d killed you. Henry said you fought them all, by yourself. There’s no way you could survive.”

Rajan wrapped an arm around her. “Well, I couldn’t let them terrorize the city, could I? You and the little one here might have been hurt.”

“I ran away and left you,” regret filled Dove’s voice.

“You went to save Eleanor. We both did what had to be done. Here, I’ve brought you food.” He pulled away from Dove and unwrapped the food. “I’m afraid it’s all squished together, but it probably still tastes good, if you don’t mind bovinder mixed with sweet fruit.”

Dove let out a cry of delight and accepted the squished sticky mess Rajan pressed into her hands.

“Where did you get this? You didn’t . . . loot it, did you? You could have been killed.”

Rajan gave some of the sweet fruit to the child. “I stole it from Lord Theodoric.”

Dove sucked in a sharp breath. “You didn’t? He’ll kill you.”

“He already planned to do that. He sentenced me to death for being a renegade Naga, but I escaped.” Rajan reached across the darkness and let his fingers linger on her cheek. "Oh, Dove. I wish I could stay here with you forever. You and Eleanor are more than I ever dreamed possible in my life, but . . ."

Dove wrapped her fingers around his. "He'll find you if you stay."

"Yes, and that would put you both in danger."

"Never mind us. You shouldn't have wasted time coming here at all. You could be long gone from the city by now. You should be."

"I know." Rajan pressed her fingers to his lips. "I know. But I'll never see you again, and I had to make sure you were all right." He closed his eyes and savored the feel of her hand in his. "I have been so alone for so long." His chest tightened, and he could no longer speak.

He felt Dove's face close to his. Her free hand slipped behind his neck and tilted his head downward so their lips met. Hers were cold and tasted of salty tears. He startled back, remembering how he'd hurt the last girl who tried to kiss him. Emotion and power shouldn't mix. He held his breath for a moment while he got his mind under control.

Dove rubbed his face. "Are you frightened?"

"Terrified," he managed to choke out. "I don't want to hurt you."

She sighed and pulled him down to lie beside her. Not resisting, he wrapped her in his arms.

Eleanor climbed over them to get more food.

"I don't think you will hurt me, and I'm tired of being cold," Dove said.

"Me too." Rajan pulled the blankets overtop of them. Her body warmed his and he radiated the heat back to her. He lay there in the dark and wondered how much time was left before the sun rose. If only he could capture a lifetime in a few moments.

"The Naga Guard will come for me," he said, running his fingers through her hair.

"I know. You should leave now."

"I will. I am. I—"

She kissed him.

He kissed her back.

"Rajan," Frederick hissed from outside the tent. "There's a dragon in the sky. It's winged over the camp twice now."

Rajan reached out with his mind and found Captain Vitra's waiting for him.

*You may have Lord Theodoric's favor, but not mine, renegade. You have broken your oath to me, and I will kill you.*

## Chapter Fifteen

**Dharanidhar landed on a jagged** outcropping overlooking the jungle. Despite the medicine Devaj had given him, his whole body ached. Not too much to fly, but enough to make both him and Kanvar uncomfortable.

"At least Parmver taught Devaj how to make your pain medication before he left the castle," Kanvar said. He'd been glad when Bensharie and Devaj had joined them in the blue dragon cove. Fearing for the safety of the villagers, Kanvar had sent Bensharie, Devaj, and Elkatran to evacuate the jungle village.

Kanvar had been unsure where the villagers could go for safety, but Devaj said he knew of a place. A safe place on the western coast of Kundiland. Kanvar was glad to hear that Eska and Denali had gotten out of the palace, taking Kumar's dog with them. Karishi, too, had gone to the village to keep Tazeran from gobbling up all the gold in the palace and to look for a wife. They'd all gone to the village for safety, not knowing that was where the combined human armies would strike.

Kanvar hoped he'd reached Kundiland in time to get them out of harm's way. He'd known the human enemies were coming, but had not expected to have to face enemies at home in the palace. He had never gotten along with Rajahansa, Haidar, and Liander, but their betrayal of his father was a dangerous distraction to deal with when the human armies were almost upon them.

Kanvar's father and mother, Parmver, Aadi, and Tana were trapped at the palace in Rajahansa's clutches. The thought of it made Kanvar's face burn with anger. Dharanidhar growled deep in his throat.

"I hope Tana's all right," Kanvar said, staring out across the tops of the trees to the distance where the golden palace clung to a cliff high above the canopy.

*I don't like to think of her stuck in the palace with Rajahansa with the way he's been acting*, Dharanidhar said. *Somehow we have to get her out as well as your parents.*

"We can't take her away from the gold dragons. How will she bond?" Kanvar wanted to see Tana again, but he was a bit nervous. Things had been so rocky between them when he'd left.

*There are other dragons beside Great Golds.* Dharanidhar flexed his wings. *Let's go get this over with. By the fountain, I hope we can sneak in through Parmver's lab without being discovered.*

"Wait, look." Kanvar directed his eyes toward the jungle. There was no wind, but the trees thrashed as if tossed by a gale. As Kanvar focused on the movement, his mind became aware of hundreds of lesser dragons and dozens of Great Dragons of various kinds gathered in the jungle below the palace.

*Rajahansa's army*, Dharanidhar said. *It may not be so easy to get in and out of there if he's placed any as guards in the palace.*

"Let's hope he hasn't." Kanvar eased his crossbow out of its harness and loaded it.

*It's foolish to fly over there,* Dharanidhar said.

"Of course." Kanvar allowed himself a grim smile.

Dharanidhar chuckled. *Which is why we're going to do it.*

"Yes," Kanvar said.

Dharanidhar flapped his great wings and took to the air, swooping down to glide just above the treetops where anyone looking out from the palace windows would be least likely to see him.

*You are blue against green trees,* Kanvar said. *They're more likely to see you against the green trees than the blue sky higher up.* He spoke directly into Dharanidhar's mind now that the rush of wind made it impossible for his friend to hear his voice.

*If they're looking down.* Dharanidhar snorted and headed for the cleft in the mountain face below the palace. He'd gotten into Parmver's lab unnoticed twice before and hoped to do so a third time. But his hopes were dashed as he got up close and found the cleft no longer there. Somehow the rock had been closed together as if the entrance to the cavern that held Parmver's lab had never been there.

Dharanidhar pulled up before he hit the cliff face. The air above them filled with Great Gold dragons who launched themselves from the palace and flew to intercept them, led by Rajahansa.

Kanvar gasped.

*Did you think I wouldn't be waiting for you?* Rajahansa said.

Dharanidhar tensed, readying for a fight, stoking his fires. He back-flapped to put space between himself and Rajahansa. The other dragons closed in around him.

*Rajahansa.* Kanvar pointed his crossbow at the Great Gold Dragon King, then lowered it, cursing. If he hurt Rajahansa, he'd hurt his father as well. *I've come for my father. You have him chained. I demand that you release him and the women to me.*

*You . . . demand?* Rajahansa laughed. *You are in no position to do any such thing.*

Kanvar gritted his teeth. *You once sent Indumauli to make sure Dharanidhar was not abusing his powers to enslave and control me. Which is why I find it hard to believe that you would turn against my father. You share a bond with him. You have been companions for hundreds of years. How could you betray him? How could you chain him? By the fountain, Rajahansa, why?*

Dharanidhar tried to maneuver out of the circle of gold dragons, but the younger ones hemmed him in. Rajahansa flared his wings and roared, revealing the wounds Anilon had given him at the blue dragon nesting grounds.

## Dragonbound V

*Your father is being punished for your crimes, Kanvar. You disobeyed me, and your actions would have doomed us to extinction if I had not found a solution.*

*You think fighting a war with the humans will solve anything? No, that is what will cause your extinction. There is still time for you to get away. I have found a place on the other side of the world where you can live in safety. I'll take you there. We can all go together.* Sweat trickled down Kanvar's face and soaked his shirt under his armor. Please, he thought to himself, please be reasonable.

*Why should I flee when I've been assured victory?*

*You can't win. There are too many humans. They have too many weapons, and they have the singing stones, so you cannot control their minds.*

Dharanidhar's wings burned from flapping to stay in one place for so long. He sucked in a heavy breath, trying to keep the pain at bay.

Rajahansa let out an exultant roar. *That is where you are wrong. Khalid has shown me a way to victory. The humans will fall before our might. The time of the Great Gold dragons is at hand. Stonefountain will rise once more.*

Kanvar's heart froze. *Khalid? You've spoken with Khalid?*

*Through the link he formed in Devaj's mind. He has assured me of victory, but I need your father to accomplish it.*

*NO!* Kanvar's mind flashed to Khalid's spirit in Stonefountain nearly consuming Devaj. Khalid only needed a Naga body to inhabit, and he would live again.

*Don't worry. You won't be around to see our triumph. My children, kill the abomination.* At Rajahansa's command, the gold dragons dove at Kanvar and Dharanidhar, filling the air with their joy breath and slashing with their claws.

*Hold your breath,* Dharanidhar told Kanvar as he blew a curtain of hot blue fire at the closest dragons. Then he dove through the flames, coming out of the fire straight into the faces of three young gold dragons. He slashed at their eyes with his claws, and the young dragons gave way.

Kanvar's lungs burned, but he refused to suck in a breath until they'd cleared the circle and flown into clean air. He got one breath, then Rajahansa descended in front of them and sprayed another gout of joy breath in their faces. At the same time he flung himself at Dharanidhar's weak wing, gouging and tearing with his claws.

Kanvar held his breath again and released his crossbow bolt at Rajahansa, aiming to wound him and not kill. Kanvar winced as the bolt sank into Rajahansa's shoulder where the wing intersected with his back.

I'm sorry father, he thought.

Rajahansa roared in pain and pulled away.

*Fly*, Kanvar told Dharanidhar. But Dharanidhar's tattered wing could not do much more than keep them in the air and advance them forward at a crawl. The gold dragons harried them, slashing and tearing at Dharanidhar, not even bothering with their joy breathe now they knew they would not need it to tear him from the sky.

Kanvar got another bolt on his crossbow and fired it, taking one of the youngsters in the chest and feeling bad when the little gold dragon squealed in pain and spun away. Kanvar looked down, hoping he hadn't killed the child.

One of the older dragons caught the young one and carried him off to treat the wound.

When Kanvar looked back up, the air was full of Great Blue dragons.

Blue fire drove the gold dragons away from Dharanidhar. A pair of blue dragons came up, one on either side, and caught Dharanidhar between them then shot away from the palace.

Kanvar turned back. *No, wait. My father. We have to save him. We have to get him away from Rajahansa.*

*Sorry. That's not what we're here for.* Anilon swept past them. The cry of Akshara's singing stone suddenly split the air, and Anilon dove toward the jungle, sweeping back and forth above the canopy while the rest of the Great Blue dragon pride engaged in aerial combat with the Great Gold dragons.

Roars from the enslaved dragons below rose up as Akshara's stone freed their minds from Rajahansa's control. The skies filled with green and tan winged raptors who trumpeted and flew away. The jungle thrashed as hundreds of other dragons rushed for freedom.

The scene receded from Kanvar's view as the dragons who supported Dharanidhar flew a straight course back to the Great Blue dragon's nesting grounds in the high mountains. Before they reached it, Anilon and the rest of the Great Blue dragon pride joined them. Akshara's stone no longer sang, and Kanvar figured Anilon must have found a new iron box to house it in.

*Anilon*, Kanvar said, *why bring us back here? Dharanidhar and I are in exile.*

*You freed us from the Great Gold Dragon King.* Anilon dropped into place to fly close beside his old mentor and friend. *Akshara is gone, but you have taken his place as Liberator. We will show you both the same respect we did him.*

Kanvar swallowed a lump in his throat. *Thank you.*

Anilon let out a satisfied puff of fire and peeled away as the dragons brought Dharanidhar down and set him on the ground in front of Akshara's lair at the Great Blue dragons nesting grounds. Behind them the lake sparkled in the sunlight.

Dharanidhar crawled inside, lay down, and started, licking his wounds. Kanvar cut the vines that bound him to Dharanidhar's neck and slid to the ground. The ancient dragon smell still clung to the cave, though Akshara's elaborately carved chests were gone from the lair.

Kanvar stretched his sore muscles. He hurt, felt Dharanidhar's pain. It would be nice to have more of Parmver's medicine, but he could not complain. The Great Blue dragons had let him and Dhar come home.

A young one hauled in a pair of dead leatherwings for Dharanidhar to eat.

*Thank you*, Dharanidhar rumbled.

A bundle of white knocked Kanvar to the ground from behind.

"Ugh, Frost," Kanvar pushed the white dragon hatchling off him.

*I missed you*, Frost said, licking his face.

"I missed you too." Kanvar gave her a hug. Anilon landed outside and Kanvar went out to meet him.

"You saved us. Thank you." Kanvar looked up into the Great Blue dragon's face.

*And you saved us. I'm sorry we could not stay to help your father. But we cannot dodge their joy breath forever. Is he truly a prisoner then?*

Kanvar slid his crossbow into the harness on his back. Rajahansa's claims terrified him.

"Anilon," he said, though he could barely choke the words out. "Rajahansa plans to return Khalid to this world, using my father's body as a vessel to hold Khalid's spirit. We have to . . . free my father from Rajahansa before he does this. Your freeing the enslaved dragons today was brilliant, but not enough. Rajahansa will just regather them. The only solution is to find a way to get my father away from Rajahansa before he frees Khalid."

Anilon bared his teeth, and fire crackled between his jaws. *We will find a way.*

"We will need the help of the other Nagas who have rebelled against Rajahansa: my brother Devaj, Karishi, and Kumar Raza's brother, Rajan. It will take all of us working together to stop this madness."

*I do not like working with Nagas.*

"I know. I'm sorry. Can you think of a way to . . . do what we must without them?"

Anilon shook his head. *Whatever it takes to prevent Khalid from returning to this world I will do.*

## Chapter Sixteen

**"Vitra's right above us.** He'll kill you to get to me." Rajan tore away from Dove, crawled out of the tent, and bolted toward the bay.

Above him, Vitra's dragon roared. Rajan wondered if gold dragons could see in the dark like red volcanic dragons could. He strengthened the shields around his mind and kept running, staying in the shadows though the edges of the sky were turning gray, dodging from one rubble pile to the next. The gold dragon swept back and forth in the sky above him. Was he searching or just letting Rajan exhaust himself before diving to finish him? If he could just get to the water and Silverwave, he'd be all right.

The smell of death and decay surrounded him, sucked into his lungs, smothering him. The crunch of his footsteps on shattered rocks, sounded loud in his ears. He stumbled over a pile of splintered wood and fell to his knees.

Overhead, the dragon roared again.

Rajan leaped back up. Even if he never made it to the water, at least he'd get as much distance between himself and Dove as he could. He'd been selfish to risk her life by coming to her. His breath came in ragged gasps as he raced across the broken city. His muscles burned. His lungs burned. His shirtsleeve caught on a pile of rubble and tore as he sped past.

*Running will not save you*, Vitra spoke into his mind.

Rajan blocked him out, not bothering to respond.

The scent of salt water cut through the cloying smell of decay.

He was close.

As he rounded a pile of rubble, the sun tipped onto the horizon and painted the bay gold.

So close.

The rubble of fallen houses gave way to broken boats and twisted planks from the shattered docks.

Rajan sucked in a breath and put on a burst of speed.

Vitra's dragon landed in front of him, blocking his path to the water.

Rajan drew his sword and sprinted left to go around.

The dragon blocked his path with a swat of his tail.

Rajan dodged the tail and changed direction to go the other way around.

The gold dragon sucked in, then sent a spurt of joy breath into Rajan's face.

Rajan held his breath and skidded down behind an upturned boat.

The dragon clawed the boat aside.

"You can't hide," Vitra shouted. "My judgment is upon you."

"Your dragon's judgment, you mean." Rajan raced out of range of the joy breath, trying to work his way around toward the beach. "You're afraid to fight me yourself, because you know I'm the better swordsman."

"You will never equal my prowess with the sword. No one beats me."

Rajan stopped running and turned to face Vitra and his dragon. "Then prove it. Come down off that ugly beast and show me you're not the coward I think you are."

Kumar's sword hilt felt warm and familiar in his hand. Not his own sword, true, but a better one. Kumar, it seemed, only carried the best of weapons. The balance was perfect, the weight just right to avoid undue muscles exhaustion. Rajan sucked in a breath, savoring the salt spray on the clean ocean breeze. The water beckoned him. It splashed, and a sliver coil appeared above the surface before slipping back out of view. Freedom lay so close, and only one man and his dragon blocked his path.

"You are beneath my skill as a swordsman," Vitra said.

"That's what I thought," Rajan said. "You're a coward. Very well. I will fight your dragon instead. Whether I kill you or him, the outcome is the same." Rajan jumped forward and drove his sword two-handed into the dragon's leg. The sword punctured the dragon's gold plate and sank into the flesh beneath. Gold dragons were so much softer than volcanic ones.

Both Vitra and his dragon roared with pain, and Rajan didn't wait for a counterattack. He pulled the sword free and raced at the dragon's stomach. He put all his weight behind a second strike that would drive the sword deep into the dragon's bowels.

The dragon lifted into the air, and Rajan slammed into the ground, his sword sinking into the gritty sand instead. The dragon sprayed the air around him with joy breath.

Tearing his sword free, Rajan held his breath and rolled away, then jumped to his feet and raced toward the water.

The dragon came down on top of him. As Rajan felt the weight of the great monster approach, he lifted the sword tip to the sky and stabbed upward.

The dragon cried out again as the sword pierced the center of his foreclaw. It lifted away and dropped to the ground beside Rajan, snapping its teeth at him, trying to catch him up in its jaws.

Rajan swung the edge of the sword against the dragon's face, chipping teeth and cutting into its muzzle. Its golden dragonstone pulsed with light as it said something to Vitra. Rajan didn't wait to see what it was, he stabbed at the dragon's eye.

The dragon reared back before the sword pierced him and blasted Rajan with another joy breath.

Rajan pivoted away and once again ran toward the water. His foot splashed into a puddle from a receding wave, and the gold dragon's tail hit him, knocking him down, pinning him. The sword flew from his hand. He gasped, but could not draw air into his lungs with the weight of the dragon on top of him.

A wave crashed into his face and then sucked back out to sea.

Sand crunched as Vitra slid down off his dragon's back and strode over to where Rajan lay pinned beneath the heavy tail.

Vitra drew his sword. "Time to sever your ugly face from the rest of your body."

Rajan spit at him and roared, clawing at the tail that held him down.

Vitra laughed and raised his sword.

A wave rolled onto the beach, breaking against the gold dragon with a crash and a hiss. The force of the water lifted the dragon's tail.

Rajan rolled free and pounced on Vitra, claws tearing at his chest, teeth biting his face, his shoulders, his neck. Vitra fell to the ground beneath the wild onslaught, crying out and trying to push Rajan off of him.

Rajan got Vitra's throat in his jaws and clamped down. Blood welled up into Rajan's mouth. A single twist of his head and Vitra's life would be over.

"Rajan." Kumar Raza's voice stopped him from tearing Vitra's throat out.

Rajan froze. His fingers closed around the hilt of Vitra's sword which had fallen onto the ground next to them.

"Let him go, little brother." Kumar's voice was calm and smooth. "Just stand up and move away."

Rajan felt Lord Theodoric and his dragon along with Kumar. Other Nagas and dragons were in the air, winging toward him. So many he could not separate all their minds into individuals. If he killed Vitra, both he and Kumar's lives would be forfeit.

He released his jaws from Vitra's throat and in the same movement pressed Vitra's sword against it instead and dragged Vitra to his feet, facing Theodoric and Kumar.

*Silverwave, get ready*, he said. He felt her in the water close by.

Rajan spit the blood from his mouth. "Good Morning, Your Lordship, Kumar. Vitra and I were just settling our differences."

"I think it's settled," Kumar said.

Theodoric's face wore a deep frown. "Let Vitra go." Lord Theodoric's mind grappled with Rajan's, trying to gain control. He was more powerful than Rajan, it wouldn't take him long.

Rajan used all his energy to keep his shields up. He just needed a moment more. He laughed. "I don't think so." He turned his attention to his brother. "Kumar, you can't show them the way to Kundiland. They will destroy the Western world."

Kumar took a deep breath and stroked his beard a moment before answering. "No. I believe they will obey the king. I know Amar. I trust him. He will let no evil come to the world because of this. Release Vitra. We will go to the king, and he will judge you fairly."

"I don't believe you." Rajan edged back into the water, dragging Vitra with him, the sword tight against his throat. The breaking waves soaked their chests.

Kumar followed him, a reassuring hand outstretched. "It's all right, Rajan. Just let him go. No one is going to hurt you. We saw what happened. Lay down the sword, and everything will be all right."

Rajan swallowed. The taste of human blood would not leave his tongue. Just a little farther, he thought to himself. Come out here, brother, and take the sword from me. He pressed the sharp blade hard against Vitra's throat, drawing more blood.

"By the fountain," Vitra cried. "Stop him, Thoedoric."

Lord Theodoric increased his efforts, shattering Rajan's shields just as Kumar made his move, diving forward and wrenching the sword away from Vitra's throat.

Rajan let it go, shoved Vitra aside, grabbed his brother instead, and dragged him down into the water.

Silverwave's coil wrapped around them both, and she shot out into the bay. Water rushed past Rajan's face in a torrent of motion. Lord Theodoric's hold on his mind slipped away.

Silverwave had recovered fully and her speed was like a crossbow bolt. She kept Rajan and Kumar under the water until his lungs felt like they would burst. Then she surfaced.

Rajan gasped for breath, blinked the water out of his eyes, and saw the sky filled with the Naga Guard, sweeping over the bay, crossbows ready. They saw him and fired.

Silverwave jerked Rajan and Kumar deep under again, switched directions and shot out farther. When she came up for them to breathe again, the army of Nagas was still searching for them in the directions she'd initially gone.

Not waiting for them to notice her change, she dove again, switching directions once more, swimming fast. Surface, dive, and switch. Surface, dive, and switch, she swam out of the bay to the reef beyond. By the time she deposited Kumar and Rajan in the shallow water on a high section of the reef, the Nagas had lost complete track of them.

In his mind, Rajan could faintly hear Vitra cursing as Lord Theodoric ordered his men to form ranks. *The renegade Naga and his brother are nothing to us,* Theodoric said. *Our loyalty is to His Majesty. We must not hesitate to fly to his aid.*

Vitra objected, but Theodoric would not be moved. The sky over the bay rippled with gold as Lord Theodoric and his army of Nagas swept away to the east.

Rajan wiped the salt water from his face. "I suppose he saw in your mind where your king is and how to get there?"

"Yes, of course," Kumar snapped. "What have you done with my sword?"

Rajan's hand went to the empty sheath at his waist. "Lost it. Sorry."

"Sorry? That's all you can say? You run off in the night. Steal from the palace. Fight with Theodoric's captain—"

"Defeat Theodoric's captain."

"Abduct me, and lose my sword! What am I going to do with you?"

Rajan laughed. "Come with me. I'd rather be a renegade than answer to a king."

Kumar grimaced. "Amar is more of a friend than a king. He is nothing like Vitra and Theodoric. You'll like him, Rajan. I promise. We need to get to Kundiland and help him. He needs me."

Rajan shivered. Here he was wet and cold again. "I don't know, Kumar. He's bound to hate me. This whole mess with the humans is my fault. I tried to take over and got them stirred up."

"It was the red dragon's fault, not yours."

Rajan wiped his mouth. He could still taste Vitra's blood. "I think a part of me is, and always will be a red dragon."

"Amar will not care. He is a very patient man."

Rajan looked down into the water. *What do you think, Silverwave? Should we go to Kundiland or find some warm beach somewhere on a deserted island?*

Silverwave's head and front legs snaked up onto the reef. She licked Kumar's face and handed him his sword she'd rescued from the water when Rajan lost it. *We go help the king. Just let me return to the bay and find a boat. There has to be some little rowboat somewhere that is sea worthy.*

Silverwave slid back into the water and swam away.

"What is her answer?" Kumar handed Rajan the sword.

Rajan sheathed it. "She agreed with you. We go to Kundiland."

Kumar cleared his throat. "Good. Well . . . I started this expedition around the world with you, I'm glad we get to finish it together."

## Chapter Seventeen

**In his mind,** Rajan followed Silverwave's progress back across the bay. A few small fishing boats had started to put out into the water, the few that had survived the great wave or been patched since. Silverwave avoided those. She had to find a boat to pull Kumar and Rajan to Kundiland in. A glance along the broken shoreline showed only wreckage. Snorting in annoyance, Silverwave dove to the bottom of the bay, where a number of boats had capsized or been sunk. She inspected one then another. Even raised to the surface those boats would never float for long.

Back on the reef, the waist deep water gradually rose as the tide came in. Rajan shivered.

"By the fountain, tell her to hurry, Rajan. We'll be swimming soon," Kumar Raza said.

"She can't find anything."

"Tell her to come back then and swim us up the coast. If we get to a safe place far enough from Aesir, we can fashion a raft."

*Silverwave.* Rajan sent his thoughts back to join Silverwave's mind.

Silverwave crawled through the rubble on the beach, trying to stay out of sight. An old fisherman who was trying to pull a tangled net from a pile of broken planking saw her. She snaked toward the water.

"Wait, please?" the fisherman called after her. "Blessed serpent, will you not help me with this net?"

Silverwave turned back and lifted her head to stare at the fisherman. His thoughts flooded into her and Rajan's minds. The fishermen of Navgarod considered the Great Silver serpents their protectors. Though the fishermen had no right to demand service from the magnificent serpents, time and again a drowning fisherman had been pulled from the ocean, lost ships had been lead back on course, and empty nets filled with swarms of fish by Great Silver serpents. Here in the East, the Great Silvers were considered the kindest and gentlest of dragons, and loved by all seafaring folk.

Silverwave blinked and ran her webbed claws down her side where the harpoons of Western fishermen had pierced her. She would have died if Kumar Raza had not saved her.

"Are you hurt?" the fisherman lifted a hand and took a step toward her. "I suppose the great wave has harmed even the sea creatures."

Silverwave shook her head, snaked across the rubble, and lifted the heavy planks off the fisherman's net.

"Thank you," he said.

She licked his face and went back to her own search.

Water swelled to Rajan's chest, and his teeth started to chatter.

"What's she doing?" Kumar said.

"She stopped to help a fisherman."

Kumar rolled his eyes.

*Hurry*, Rajan told Silverwave. *I don't think I'm strong enough to swim for very long.*

Silverwave crawled into an overturned boat, saw a large gash in the bottom and crawled back out. *I think everything that can put out on the water is already out there. These humans need food. They've gone to fish.*

*All right. Just grab a plank that Kumar and I can hold onto while you tow us farther up the coast.*

Snorting, Silverwave grabbed a broken plank from what once had been the dock and hauled it toward the water. Two human men mounted the line of wreckage carrying a four-man canoe on their shoulders.

As they stepped onto the sand, one of the men faltered and nearly dropped his end.

"It's all right, Henry, just set the boat down there," a woman said.

The two men lowered the boat to the ground, and Rajan saw through Silverwave's eyes that the men were Frederick and Henry. Dear Henry, carrying a boat despite his wounds.

Dove climbed over the wreckage with Eleanor in her arms. "Thank you both," she said. "I think I can push it out from here."

Rajan gasped in surprise. What was Dove doing?

"Are you sure about this?" Frederick asked.

"Yes, I'm sure. He ran this way, I saw him. He fought with Captain Vitra and then . . . a silver serpent took him into the water."

"He's dead then," Frederick rubbed his hand through his muddy hair.

"No. The Great Silver serpents are . . . it wouldn't hurt him."

"Whatever you say. You're the fisherman's daughter. But if you don't find him out there, come back to camp, all right."

"Of course. Though I'll bring in some fish first. I can't believe that of all our family's boats, only the canoe survived." Dove set her daughter into the boat beside the cloak full of food Rajan had brought her, several water gourds, and other supplies. The stolen bedding was spread across the bottom. With Eleanor secure in the boat, Dove pressed her shoulder against it to push it out into the water.

Frederick and Henry pushed as well, but Henry faltered again and fell to his knees.

*Silverwave, Henry's hurt. Can you lick his wounds?* Rajan said. His heart was tumbling like whitewater against the shore. Dove had seen him go under. She was coming to look for him. He sucked in a wavering breath and started to swim.

"Are you all right?" Kumar asked.

Rajan wiped the salt water from his eyes and only succeeded in wetting them more. "My body is numb. I don't think I can swim for long."

"Just relax and only use enough energy to keep your head above water."

"But she's coming for me," he said with a choked voice.

"Of course. Silverwave would never let you drown, and neither would I." Kumar gave him a reassuring pat on the shoulder.

Silverwave snaked over the wreckage to the humans. They froze as she came up to them. Silverwave wrapped a forearm around Henry and gently lowered him to the ground.

"Hey, get away from him," Frederick shouted. He lunged at Silverwave, but Dove grabbed him.

Silverwave ignored them. Keeping the struggling Henry pinned, she eased his tattered shirt aside, cut his bandages away with her sharp claws, and licked his wounds.

Henry stilled.

"See, she's healed him," Dove said.

"Dragon. Pretty dragon." Eleanor reached out from the boat toward Silverwave.

Silverwave snaked her head over and let the child wrap her arms around her neck.

Rajan gasped, got water in his mouth, and started choking.

"It's all right." Kumar wrapped an arm across his chest and eased him on his back so Kumar's strength could keep him afloat.

Rajan panicked and tried to get away.

"No. Don't fight me. Just relax. Float. You'll be fine until Silverwave gets back here."

"I-I'm all right. You don't understand." His brother would never know what it was like to be a Naga, to feel himself in another body. To be more than human. To be dragon.

"Don't understand what?"

The lump in Rajan's throat was too tight to let him answer as Dove spoke to Silverwave. "Do you know where Rajan is?"

Silverwave nodded.

"You're his dragon, aren't you?"

Silverwave nodded again and motioned Dove into the boat.

"Will you take me to him?"

Silverwave licked Dove's face then picked her up and set her in the boat.

"Goodbye." Frederick hugged her.

Henry got to his feet and bid her farewell also.

"Look after my sister, both of you."

The men agreed.

Dove sat down and put her daughter on her lap. Silverwave grabbed a stray length of rope from the wreckage, tied it to the oarlocks, then raced for the water, pulling the little canoe behind her.

Dove's daughter squealed as it hit the waves and water sprayed up in her face.

Rajan closed his eyes. His body was numb. He wasn't sure he'd ever get used to being this cold, but somewhere in the world there had to be water warm enough for him to enjoy it along with Silverwave. For now, he lay back and let Kumar help him float until the canoe came up beside him and Dove's worried voice snapped his eyes open.

"Rajan." Her hand closed around his arm.

He tried to reach up and pull himself into the boat, but his body was too numb. Silverwave lifted him over the side, followed by Kumar.

Dove enveloped him in a warm hug. She pulled back. "Rajan, you're frozen. Take those wet clothes off right now. She got his shirt unfastened and pulled it off him. He shivered as the cold wind hit his bare chest. But a moment later she had the cloak wrapped around him.

"It's a bit sticky on the outside and smells like roasted bovinder, but it should keep you warm and keep the sun from burning you. You're skin is so pale," Dove said as she fastened the cloak around his neck.

Rajan laughed and settled down onto the floor of the boat with his back against one of the seats.

"Da." Eleanor jumped into his arms and rubbed his chin. "Da. Da."

"Yes, I shaved." He kissed her little hand.

Kumar cleared his throat and sat down on the bench across from him. "How about some introductions here. I'm Kumar Raza. You already seem to know my brother, Rajan. Who, my darling, are you?" he said to Dove.

Dove sat down next to Rajan and leaned against his chest, letting him put his arm around her. "My name is Dove. Rajan rescued my daughter and me after the earthquake. He rescued a lot of people, actually. He was so obsessed about it, and I didn't understand why until I saw the silver dragon. Silver dragons rescue people. That's what they do. They are the kindest, gentlest creatures in the world."

Kumar grinned. "Yes, they are."

Rajan's heart stuck in his throat. He thought of all the humans trapped and tormented in the red dragon's cages. He'd never helped them. He'd hurt them and worse . . . eaten them. He doubted Dove would still care for him if she knew that, but he could find no words to tell her. "You said you saw me fight Captain Vitra. How can you think I'm as gentle as a silver dragon?"

"Vitra forced you into that. Even a silver dragon will fight when it's forced to. You could have killed Vitra, but you didn't."

"I wanted to."

Dove eased her hand beneath the cloak and rested it against his chest, her fingers warm and soothing. "I do not think you are capable of such a thing."

Rajan pulled away and jumped to his feet. "You don't know me. You know nothing about my life."

"Da," Eleanor said, hugging his leg.

"True. I only know what I've seen you do here. But from what I've seen, you are very much a silver dragon," Dove said.

Rajan shook his head.

Kumar stroked his beard and looked up at Rajan. "You can't change what has happened in the past, little brother. But you need to stop blaming yourself. The red dragon is to blame, and he alone. Dove is right. You are bound to a Great Silver serpent now. For the first time, you've had the chance to live your life the way you want to, and all you've done is serve others. What you were before has nothing to do with who you are now, what you truly are in your heart."

Rajan shivered and wrapped the cloak tighter around him. The boat crested a wave and came down hard, upsetting his balance. He dropped down beside Dove before he ended up back in the water. Perhaps Kumar was right. In truth, the red dragon had never given him any choice. Though he was not locked in the cages with the other humans, the dragon had kept his mind locked up more. Never even allowing a stray human thought or feeling. His red dragon self had not really been him. The red dragon was someone else entirely. Though the link to the red dragon was gone, he was sure some of the red dragon tendencies would always be with him. But he could overcome that. He had overcome that.

He lifted Eleanor into his lap and held her warm body to him. She wrapped her arms around his neck and kissed his cheek, sending a different kind of warmth through him than he'd felt in the heat of the dragon's lair.

"Yes. I think you are right. I am a silver dragon," he said, putting an arm around Dove. He felt whole and good and happy. "Dove," he said. "Kumar and I are from the Western world and are going back there. Do you want to come with us, or should I have Silverwave swim you back to shore. I suppose you'll want to keep your boat if you stay though." Rajan frowned.

Dove laughed and laid her head against his chest. "I have nothing to go back to in the city."

"Your sister."

"She doesn't need me. Her husband is still alive. I'd only be a burden to her."

Rajan lifted his eyes to Kumar. "Can Dove and Eleanor come with us?"

"Of course they can come," Kumar chuckled. "This is her boat after all, the only possession she has left, from the sound of it."

Rajan sighed and closed his eyes. He did not know what the future would bring. Despite Kumar's reassurance, he feared what Theodoric and his Naga Guard would do once they reached Kundiland. But for that one moment with Eleanor on his lap, his arm around Dove, and his brother close by, he felt at peace.

# About The Author

**Rebecca Shelley** (Rebecca Lyn Shelley) is the author of over 30 published books including the bestselling **Smart-boys Club** series as well as the popular **Red Dragon Codex** and **Brass Dragon Codex**. She loves writing about dragons and is excited to be writing the **Dragonbound** series. Her **Aos Si** ***trilogy*** will thrill fans of YA Paranormal Romance. To learn more or contact her, visit her website http://www.rebeccashelley.com.

If you have enjoyed reading **Dragonbound V: Silver Dragon**, Rebecca would love to have you post a review on the site where you purchased it.

## Acknowledgements

I'd like to thank all the great beta readers who helped make this book better: Abigail, Matthew, Kimberly, Emily, Harmony, Mary, and Devin. It wouldn't be what it is without your valuable feedback. Thanks also to my husband, Dave, for his continuing support. And to all my writer friends for their encouragment and example.

## Coming Soon:

BESTSELLING AUTHOR
Rebecca Shelley
Green Dragon
DRAGONBOUND VI

## Dragonbound VI: Green Dragon Preview

By Rebecca Shelley

### Chapter One

**Tana carried the breakfast** tray into the king's chambers. Unlike so many other of the Nagas, his room was his own, completely separate from his dragon's. It was big enough, for all that. Four of the village huts could easily fit inside it. Tana stepped gingerly on the plush red rug that covered the floor. It made her nervous walking on something so moss-like. Mani, the queen, sat on the bed that's frame was shaped like a silver serpent leaping from ocean waves. Her vacant eyes stared at the picture of herself on the wall across from her, but she saw nothing. Liander sat next to her, a sharp jungle knife clutched in his hand. That meant Rajahansa was still sleeping.

"Good morning, Your Majesties." Tana set the tray on the table next to the bed.

Liander leaned over and grabbed a sweet cake off the tray. "It's about time. I'm starving."

His Majesty, King Amar, stirred in his spot by the wall. Chains clanked as he rose to his feet. Chains with no lock or key. The shackles that had been fused around Amar's wrists with Naga power and secured the same way to the palace wall. The chains held him away from his wife with barely enough room to stand or sit. While Rajahansa was awake, the dragon's mind blocked Amar from using his own power to free himself from the chains. While Rajahansa slept, Liander's knife, hovering over Mani, kept him equally bound.

"Good Morning, Tana. Are you well?" Amar's white shirt was wrinkled, his gold pants stained. His face gaunt from the daily mental battles he fought with his dragon.

"I am well, thank you." Tana's eyes stung.

Amar frowned as she took him his plate of fruit and sweet cakes. "From the bleak look in your eyes, I see that you are still unhappy here at the palace."

"How can I be happy with you chained like this?" She turned a glare on Liander.

Liander stood, fingering the knife. His gaze was cold on her. "Silence, Girl. You bring the food. You keep your mouth shut. Or I'll shut it for you."

Heat rose to Tana's face. "You aren't man enough to even touch me."

"No?" Liander grabbed her, dragged her up against his chest, and forced his lips down onto her own.

The stale scent of his sweat, mixed with the taste of sweet cake on his mouth, made her gag. She struggled in his grasp, but the cold edge of the hunting knife against the back of her neck stilled her.

"Liander, stop!" Amar shouted. Chains rattled as he tugged at them, then went silent.

Liander left off kissing her and swung her around so he could press the blade hard against her throat. The king had manipulated the metal of one of the shackles, freeing his right hand.

"Put the shackle back on," Liander said, "or I'll kill her."

"You won't kill her. You need her." Amar got his other arm free.

"But we don't need your wife."

Both men stood unmoving, gauging the distance between each of them and Mani, wondering which of them could reach her first. Mani gave no notice of either man. Haidar had stripped her mind of free will, leaving her nothing more than a shell. She could not even feed herself. Tana had to do it.

Liander moved. Amar lunged, tackling Liander just before his knife would have struck Mani. The two men hit the floor, wrestling for the knife.

A roar from Rajahansa rattled the bookshelves. The Great Gold dragon appeared at the window, coming into view as he left behind the sunlight, landed on the sill, and forced his neck, chest, and forearms inside the room. He flicked Liander aside, grabbed Amar, lifted him into the air and shook him. His gold dragonstone flashed as dragon and Naga battled with each other mind-to-mind.

Liander climbed to his feet and went over to Mani, pressing the tip of the knife against her tender flesh.

Rajahansa dropped Amar next to the wall where his chains waited.

"Put the chains back on," Liander ordered.

Amar rubbed his head. His chest heaved as if he'd fought a physical battle against a dozen men. "All right," he said when he'd drawn enough air into his lungs to speak. "I'll do it. Don't hurt her. Just . . . by the fountain, leave the women alone. They should be treated with respect and care. Whatever is wrong between us, don't take it out on the women."

Rajahansa slapped the shackles back on Amar's arms and manipulated the metal to lock them there. Then he withdrew from the window and flapped away.

Amar slumped to the ground and put his head in his hands, exhausted beyond any more use of his power.

"Get out," Liander ordered Tana.

Tana took a step backwards toward the door. "But I haven't feed Mani yet."

Liander's face twisted into a cruel smile. "Don't worry. I can make her eat." He touched the side of her forehead, and Mani's arm jerked up and reached for the tray of food.

Amar choked back a quiet sob.

Tana turned and ran from the room. She rushed down the hall, passing tapestries and paintings of dragons and men, arched doorways and chambers hung with jeweled chandeliers, alcoves with statues of dragons and their Nagas. She would trade all the wealth and grandeur of the castle for one more day at home in her little wooden hut. One more day of freedom.

This was Kanvar's fault. He'd promised not to tell anyone about her connections with the dragons and a moment later broken his promise. For her own welfare, of course, because she'd die if she didn't bond with a dragon, and he'd been sure she'd be safe and happy at the palace, confident in the kind nature of his father and brother. Such a sweet family, and no man more gentle than Amar, and no one more gallant and polite as Devaj.

Tana half-smiled at the thought of Devaj, certainly no other man was as handsome as him. And Kanvar, her betrayer, her savior from both Great Green and red volcanic dragon, her friend. Maybe more. The last time they'd seen each other he had held her, kissed her forehead. Devaj was all cool gold, gentle and thoughtful, while Kanvar was fire and anger and passion. Her heart was torn between the two brothers, not that Devaj had made any move to claim her. But now they were both gone and the king chained, the palace had become a prison. Hadn't Kanvar called it that? Yes, and she'd told him it was beautiful. And it was, for a short while, before everything came crashing down.

Tana had almost reached her own chambers when Haidar's voice cut through the hall. "You're up early."

His voice gave her cold chills. "I had to feed the queen since you destroyed her mind."

"Oh, Tana. I didn't destroy it. I just tucked it away for a while. We can't have her causing trouble." Haidar put a reassuring hand on Tana's shoulder.

She'd sooner be touched by a mud toad. "Leave me alone." She shrugged his hand off, but he grabbed her arm instead.

"Don't pull away from me. You know I love you."

"You don't know what love is."

"Yes, I do." He caressed her cheek with his other hand. "It's what you and I will have as we replenish the pure Naga race."

Tana didn't try to pull away again. He could hold her with his hand or with his mind, either way she had no escape from Haidar. She rubbed her hand across her bruised lips. "Liander might object to that. He seems to have claimed me for himself."

"Nonsense. I'm the older brother. You're mine by right."

"What right? This has nothing to do with your rights. My right is to choose whatever man I wish to marry, or none at all if I want to remain single. You cannot force me to accept you as husband."

"Can't I? And who's going to stop me? Amar is powerless. My father is a weak old fool. Liander wouldn't dare cross me. I had on older brother once who might have, but he is dead, killed by the humans he tried to befriend."

"Kanvar will stop you."

Haidar snorted. "Kanvar is a walking dead man. His dragon will not survive much longer without Parmver's medicine. He can't fly, which means he can't hunt, which means he can't eat. He's doomed to a slow death by starvation if the other blue dragons don't find him first and give him the swifter option."

Tana shuddered. Kanvar had not mentioned anything to her about his dragon not being able to fly.

"Oh, don't worry." Haidar ran his hand down the full length of her braid, his fingers brushing down her back to her waist and his hand resting there. "I'll be very gentle with you. And you will love me. I promise." His mind, like his hand, caressed her thoughts, igniting a longing in her. "See. You will enjoy your life with me."

He pulled away from her, leaving her flushed and out of breath, thoughts of Kanvar flown from her mind.

Haidar pressed a hand against her forehead. "Well, you don't feel hot yet. But don't worry, I'm sure the fever will be upon you soon. You have been spending plenty of time with the dragons Rajahansa has chosen for you to pick from. The touch of the gold dragons will speed your need to bond. And on the day that you bond, we will marry."

He kissed her cheek. "Good day, my love."

Footsteps echoed down the golden hall as he walked away.

Choking back tears, Tana hurried into her chambers and locked the door behind her. Not that the lock would stop anyone in the palace besides Aadi.

"I hate him," Tana mumbled under her breath as she slumped on the bed and picked up her sewing. "I hate them both. Not sure which I hate more." Liander with his brutality or Haidar with his subtle cruelty. How could the sons of such a sweet old man be so rotten?

Her hands shook, making it hard for her to thread the needle. A few more stitches and she'd be finished with the robe she would wear for her Bonding Ceremony. She'd already suffered through three Choosing Ceremonies, being forced to look into the minds and hearts of gold dragons who were loyal to Rajahansa. He only allowed her around those who shared his thirst for the restoration of Stone-fountain and the Nagas return to power over the human world. She could not be sure if he had twisted their minds to this thinking or if they had come by the desires naturally. But it sickened her what they were willing to do, already planning in their minds and hearts, to regain domination for the Great Gold dragons.

She had chosen none of them, and Rajahansa had grown more and more angry with her.

She got the needle threaded finally and paused to scratch the itch on her chest which had grown more persistent each passing day. Parmver's ointment had helped stopped the spread of the rash so far, but she didn't know for how long. Not long enough. This robe would have to be finished today.

Shivering with a sudden chill, she set to work and did not stop until Aadi came to her door. She could tell his knock from the others. His was more of a question instead of a demand.

"Just a moment." She slid the last wooden dowel, stolen from various tapestries in her room and other inconspicuous places around the palace, into place and sewed it in.

Aadi knocked again. "Tana, open up. It's time for our training with Parmver."

"All right. I'm coming." Tana set the robe aside and returned the needle to the pincushion. The garment was ready. She could only hope it would work the way she intended it to.

# Other Books by Rebecca Shelley

## Aos Si Trilogy

## Middle Grade Fantasy

# YA Fantasy

When the only power left in the world is Death
Fairy Tome
Rebecca Shelley

Nook Children's Best-Selling Author
EBON BLADE
THE BLADE WILL
CLAIM YOUR SOUL
REBECCA
SHELLEY

TABLET OF
DESTINIES
Best-Selling Author
REBECCA SHELLEY

## Epic Fantasy Romance

## Epic Fantasy